C000138984

The History of Our World
beyond the Wave

The History of Our World beyond the Wave

A FANTASY

R. E. Klein

Harcourt Brace & Company

New York   San Diego   London

Copyright © 1998 by Robert Klein

All rights reserved. No part of this publication may be reproduced or transmitted in
any form or by any means, electronic or mechanical, including photocopy, recording,
or any information storage and retrieval system, without permission in writing from
the publisher.

Requests for permission to make copies of any part of the work should be mailed to:
Permissions Department, Harcourt Brace & Company, 6277 Sea Harbor Drive,
Orlando, Florida 32887-6777.

Library of Congress Cataloging-in-Publication Data
Klein, Robert
The history of our world beyond the wave: a fantasy/
Robert Klein.
p.   cm.
ISBN 0-15-100411-0
I. Title.
PS3561.L358H5   1998
813'.54—dc21   98-15813

Illustrations by Fiona King
Designed by Judythe Sieck
Printed in the United States of America
First edition
E D C B A

To *my* Mary
and to my friend Andy Kovats

CONTENTS

PART ONE:
The Wave

PART TWO:
The World

PART ONE:

The Wave

A Day at the Beach

 henever the world starts to worry me, I escape to the beach. The salt water helps dissolve the accumulated outrage built up by things like work and politics and other people's short-comings. You might say the ocean has a way of laundering the soul.

Laundering? My soul needed at least a washboard scrubbing as I rounded the curves of the coast highway that first day of summer, morally enervated from scoring exams and grading term papers and having to explain tactfully to students who absolutely had to have an A. I had no sympathy, not even with the world.

The sun glittering off the ocean nearly blinded me as I looked for parking along the beach front. I shielded my eyes against the glare while searching for a space, but the rest of southern California had got there before me, so I had to park half a mile from the water. I did not mind.

I did not mind much, pulling out my book and beach towel. As

Paul Sant the teacher, I had minded too much. But I was done with the semester. Now I was only Paul Sant the summer idler, eager like the rest for sand and sunlight. I slammed the trunk closed and walked toward the beach.

The streets erupted with bathers, noisy, scantily clad: rowdy young men blowing off animal energy; teenaged beauties unfurling recent curves; bag-thighed grannies, indifferent to all but cards and paperback novels; hairy-backed roués stiffly parading the ruins of ancient muscles; housewives, still pretty, but shapeless from too much marriage, dragging towheaded, spindly children—too many people, afflicting the world with noise and empty gestures. I marveled at the difference between these and the heroic inhabitants of the books I taught. Where in real life was the high romance, the spiritual conviction of Milton and Malory?

Two blocks from the beach I stopped in front of the marine warehouse, one of those colossal old places once designated as bomb shelters. Someone was renting surf mats, and I had not seen a surf mat in years. Leaning colorfully along the front of the building, they spoke eloquently of the expectation and excitement of past summers. What though the promise was never realized? Here in miniature was romance of a sort. On an impulse I selected a bright blue one, inflated and hard, raised it onto my shoulder, and went inside to pay.

"I haven't ridden one of these since high school," I told the man behind the counter, a bald, skinny fellow with a pathetic mustache.

"You never outgrow them," he said. He started to say more, but I could not hear because people were yelling outside.

"Sounds like a fight," I said, taking out my money.

"Hold on." He stepped outside to investigate. The other customers followed him. I was left alone.

Shrill, breathless screams violated the summer air. I stepped to the doorway.

People mobbed the street, screaming—stampeding—their necks craned back even as they ran, colliding with others, stumbling and falling in bunches. I looked out to sea, and my knees gave way.

My first thought was of a knife across the horizon, curved and sharp like a scimitar; then it was higher and nearer, and it was more like a wall in motion, then a mountain range shining with sunlight, its craggy peaks shifting and regrouping as the mountain expanded. Then it was like the sky, as high as the stars and hissing, and I had to crane my head way back because its crest rose over the sun. The tidal wave was all.

Someone crashed into me, sent me sprawling back inside the warehouse. Still clutching the canvas raft, I fled down the stairs to a storage room and rolled the steel door shut behind me.

For a moment all was still. A square of warm sunlight shone through the big skylight in the center of the immense room, illuminating crates of hardware, gauges and valves, diving apparatus for the summer season. The overhead lights were on, too. Nearby, against the wall, was a rack of scuba tanks with regulators attached. They were all set up and ready to bring upstairs. The only sound was my breathing.

The skylight went dark just before it exploded in a concussion that knocked out the lights and threw me to the cement floor. Water hit me. I tried to rise. The current was knee-high, waist-high. I was swept along. Drowning. My hand felt rounded metal. A scuba tank. I held on—got the mouthpiece in and turned on the air. I choked, racked with coughs, till my breathing passages cleared. I nearly swooned to the luxury of breathable air. In my mouth, out my nostrils. I was alive, and I could breathe. I was completely submerged, but I wasn't going to drown.

The churning waters tried to pull me away, but I doggedly held on—managing to wedge myself between the rack and the wall. I was terribly cold, I had no sight, and the water felt oppressively heavy, but I could breathe. Sooner or later the wave would spend itself and flow back to the sea, and I could swim out. I had to endure till then or be drowned by deadly currents or sucked to sea by the retreating wave. I wondered how far inland it would travel. When would it drain back? And what of all the people? So I crouched shivering beneath the weight of water, pondering the wave that had swept over the warehouse, bursting the skylight, pouring in from all sides. Now and then gurgling sounds interrupted the dead silence as pockets of air broke loose. After a long while these ceased, and the stillness was complete except for my breathing. I knew it was time to swim out.

I released my legs from the space between the rack and the wall, but my legs did not respond, so I kneaded them until they did what they were supposed to. Then I slipped the scuba tank out of the rack and under my arm, and swam to where I remembered the railing was that led to the steel door.

The door was jammed shut. No matter how hard I tried, I could not move it. I tugged and pushed, even hammered with the scuba tank till I left off exhausted.

I found my way back to my old spot between the wall and the scuba rack and settled in once more, secure in the feel of the metal tubes. I would stop long enough to catch my breath and change tanks, then try the door again. I switched over to another tank, but the effort left me suddenly sleepy. I could rest awhile. I had plenty of air. The door was a few feet away. I would try in a moment or two. Instead, I lingered inhaling oxygen till I felt so comfortable and light-headed, I could have slept. The voices came eventually.

Paul Sant is down here, someone said.

Is he alone? asked another voice.

No, the first voice said. We are down here too.

Who are you?

We are the drowned.

We hunt for Paul Sant, said a different voice.

Why?

We have use for him.

Where is Paul? a new voice said. Our mouths fly open to know his hiding place.

We want to stroke him with our palpy fingers.

We want to show him our new faces.

"Don't tell them where I am!" I pleaded.

Ah, he hides drinking oxygen by the rack of scuba tanks. Open your eyes, Paul, and see your friends.

I looked into green faces—the mouths opening and closing, opening and closing.

Hallucination! I cried. I jammed my fists into my eyes, and rubbed until my brain exploded into bright sparks. I opened my eyes, but another eye was watching. The faces were gone, but the eye would not go away—glaring white, without a pupil—blind, yet watching, watching. Abruptly I knew I was looking at the sun shining through the broken skylight.

I had forgotten the skylight. Clutching the tank under one arm, I filled my lungs, kicked out, and swam for the faint light overhead.

Upward I swam, and upward still, though my arms ached with the effort and my heart seemed to kick at my chest. In a kind of fury I shut my eyes and flailed.

Something solid waited for me, just before the skylight. I tried to crawl around it, climb over it, shoulder it aside. My body became fouled in rope. I kicked out, and the object and I shot through the skylight and were fired high through murky waters.

Up and up, still clutching the scuba tank, rising with the pressure singing in my ears, I streaked upward, rising as though I were a million fathoms down, rising through gloomy waters as if rising were all I ever intended to do, rising till I had been rising all my life, rising till the pressure took my head off.

All of a sudden I broke the surface, the scuba tank torn from my grasp, my numb hands clutching hard inflated canvas. I had found my surf mat, and it had carried me all the way up.

I was on my surf mat in the bright sunlight, with ocean all around me as far as I could see.

Afloat

t took a while before my eyes adapted
to the bright sunlight, but there was
nothing to see but ocean. I floated
comfortably above the water, the sun straight overhead. Someone
would come by in an aircraft or boat, and I was in plain sight. The
sun on my back baked the sea chill from my bones. Someone would
come along. A wave of sleep overcame me, and I dozed, then
sprang awake. The sea stretched broad and flat, with the tiniest of
swells gently lifting and lowering me. I closed my eyes once more.
I must have slept long, because when I awoke to the shock of cold
water washing over me, the sun was low in the sky. I bounced along
short, choppy waves, the air thick with spray.

The tide suddenly lurched forward. I gripped the sides of the surf
mat tightly to avoid having it pulled out from under me. The current moved so fast, I had to lower most of my body behind the
mat to counterbalance the forward movement.

The setting sun at my back, I shot through the water, heading east, bits of wreckage floating about me in the current, things prosaic enough in themselves, but as flotsam incongruous and grotesque, all fitfully alight in the sun's last rays.

On I sped, soaked and stiff with cold, yet exhilarated by the speed and elated at the conviction that sooner or later I must touch land. Still, I wondered how I had got so far out to sea.

By the time night set in, my body was so numb, I could no longer feel the canvas mat. But my grip did not loosen. I looked up to search the sky. No moon had risen to light my way. A few stars glittered with a faint metallic lustre.

The night wore on, cold and dark. Soon would come light, and there would be land, and someone would give me water to drink and a warm bed to lie in. My eyes snapped open.

If I slept, I would probably lose the surf mat and drown. I tried to talk myself awake, but my throat was dry with thirst. That is what will get me to land, I thought to the waves and the current and to the aluminum stars overhead. Thirst will get me to land. It took no effort. I had only to open my mouth to the air. Thirst did the rest.

Only yesterday—was it yesterday? or maybe the day before—I rented a surf mat at the beach to float among the waves. Now I floated indeed. I laughed out loud, and my thirst laughed with me.

Something glowed up ahead—either the light of morning or the sun in my throat; I could not be sure which. I closed my eyes and tried to taste the cold drink I would have just before I sank down into my warm soft bed.

Open your eyes.

The top of the sun rose just ahead. A dark mass loomed in the distance, to my left.

Turn, said the throat. Leave the current, or be swept past the landmass that rises like a dark mountain. Paddle with your hands.

I tried to shift my body upward to free my hands for paddling, but my body ignored me.

Concentrate. You can see your hands now. Your legs are there too, in the water, even if you can't see them. Hurry and turn, or you will lose the land.

I called out with all the thirst I had. Sparks shot from my throat to my chest, through both arms, and down to the legs I knew were somewhere in the water. Arching slightly, I pulled the surf mat deeply under me, hugging the edges with the insides of my arms. I could paddle now. I could kick as well.

I skimmed along at an angle to the current's edge, which was marked by a turbulence, then a flattening of the waves. Then I was through it, calmly bobbing on a quiet sea. Now I paddled in earnest, taking long, sure strokes, my feet churning like an outboard motor. All the while the sky filled with light.

The land took on definite shape. There was no beach, just a forest of pines stretching down to the water. More strokes, and I was weaving in and out of submerged treetops. Just ahead the water lapped gently against a slope of solid earth.

My feet touched bottom. I dragged the mat high up the bank onto a dry bed of pine needles, my legs giving way almost constantly. Yet the mat was safe, and I could stand, after a fashion. I stood at the bottom of a hill. Above me was a cabin.

I found strength to trudge up the hill and bang on the cabin door. I did not wait for an answer but walked into a big general room with beds against two walls, and an adjoining kitchen. In the kitchen was a sink. I lurched over and turned the tap. Water spilled out. An empty glass stood on the counter. I drank.

I staggered over to a bed, climbed in, and pulled the covers up. At last I slept beneath warm blankets.

CHAPTER 3

Where Are the People?

 found cans of meat and vegetables. There was also a wood-burning stove. Next to the sink was a refrigerator filled with perishable goods, but the electricity was off and the food in ruins. I rested some time, eating the canned goods and drinking the cold water which flowed from a tank behind the cabin. And I found all the clothes I needed. What has happened to the world? I asked the oaken beams, pine panelling, and cedar bedposts. Where has the Wave brought me? But no one came to give the answers.

One morning I felt strong enough to leave the cabin. I walked into the bright sunshine and followed a dirt path, which twisted inland. The weather was hot, the forest awash with the heady scent of pine. Raucous birds screamed in the trees. A big gray squirrel scampered away in a flurry of bushed tail.

The path took me around to the far west, switchbacked higher, spiraling inland till I lost sight of the sea, then turned sharply in front of a porch of a big shingle house.

I called, then climbed the wooden steps and knocked firmly on the door. I waited, knocked again, went around to a window, and returned to try the door. It was locked. Just down the road were more cabins.

"Hello!" I shouted. "Where is everybody?" I banged on doors, rattled each knob, pushed each bell.

All was silent, locked and deserted.

I climbed higher up the path and looked down upon the sea. An A-frame roof protruded from the lapping waters. Farther on I found other drowned cabins. I wandered higher till the path ended, clambered up a peak, and saw I was on an island. Just across the bay were other peaks, brown and empty, rising from a motionless sea.

I spent the day looking for other people. The island must have been five or six miles in circumference, its highest parts steep and inaccessible, its gentler slopes studded with resort cabins stretching to the sea. All the cabins were silent and empty. I was the only one on the island.

I returned to what I regarded as my cabin, and that night after a hot meal I lit the Coleman lanterns and looked for something to read. But I found nothing besides Stoddard *On the Steam Engine,* which I quickly put down. I must survive till rescue comes, I said to the lanterns and wood-burning stove. But when could it reasonably come? I tried to calculate the days, but the days were impossible to figure; that summer morning of the Wave already seemed an epoch of the past. I thought back to the surge of noisy bathers going toward the beach. I would give anything to have them now.

Next morning I walked down to the ocean. The first thing was to survive. The second was to be ready when people came. I thought of converting one whole cabin into a signal flare by stockpiling there the barrels of coal oil that I found stored in everyone's supply bin, to be touched off the moment I saw a plane or ship. But I felt a curious disinclination to violate any of the cabins, so turned instead to build a woodpile. I prowled the shore for driftwood.

The coastline was ragged with inlets and narrow, shallow coves. The sea ran high, shooting bursts of spray among the great lichenous boulders that stood far above the shoreline. Everywhere a fringe of drowned trees skirted the land like pilings from an unfinished pier. I looked for my surf mat, but it must have washed away.

I followed the coast in search of driftwood but found only kindling for my pains, until, entering a cove, I nearly fell over a surfeit of wood partly beached and partly floating in shallow water. It was a platform, perfectly flat and perfectly square, fashioned of immense black timbers crudely hewn and held together by an arrangement of wooden pegs. The platform was easily a hundred feet on a side, and so large and stable that it barely moved in the restless sea. I returned for rope to tie it down and felt secure for lumber.

That night something disturbed the silence outside my window, not with the ordinary noise one expects in a forest, but a sort of *click . . . click . . . click.* I peered out but could see nothing.

The cabin shook next morning as mountains of water boomed high into the pines. I ran outside to witness the ocean erupting into whirlpools and clamorous tides, sometimes like a gusher launching black mud far onto shore. The phenomenon lasted till midday; then the sea slept once more, and I continued to explore the island and my own thoughts. The worst part of my solitary existence thus far had been the loneliness. Now came a disquieting revelation of self-knowledge. Since the Wave I'd had few thoughts but for survival. There was leisure now, as I hiked along, to mourn the loss of all who fell beneath the Wave. I thought of all the drowned and displaced, all those whose loss was far greater than mine. I thought about them as I walked the switchbacks. And I was disturbed that I didn't care.

In the evening after dinner I heard once more the click... *click*... *click*. Slowly, very slowly, I stepped to the window and drew back the curtains. There was only the silver glory of the sea. The sea was on fire with moonlight, and empty, quite empty. The rippling waters burned as with a million electric snakes.

CHAPTER 4

The Tug-of-War

 put off dismantling the platform because of the storms. Both day and night the lightning sizzled, and the rain thudded on the cabin roof in fat, thick drops, growing more and more violent till lashed to missiles by the horrific wind stalking through the forest like a prehistoric beast. And amid the roar resounded a deeper note as the surf boomed high among the trees near the cabin. The cabin groaned with every burst of wind while through the window I watched the flood merge with the thrashing sea. Day after day after day.

One morning all was still. Armed with a crowbar and saw, I left to build my woodpile from the floating platform. The dirt path outside the cabin had turned to ooze; the trees dripped monotonously. Secure in its cove, the platform stretched wet and stable like a polished dance floor on the rocking waves, its wealth of timber awaiting. But I dared not approach the water.

The sea bristled with triangular fins rising several feet above the waves. I knew whales; whales spouted and dove headfirst, brandishing their flukes till the flukes stood straight up out of the water. I knew whales. These were not whales.

For three days the fins dominated the turbulent waters. Then they vanished.

Still I was reluctant to strip the platform of its timber. Another storm was on the way. The day had been bitter and sultry, the sky charged with electricity. By afternoon, flashes of sheet lightning exploded like bombs across the northern sky.

I was down by the beach in one of the innumerable inlets, setting lines in hopes of catching something before the storm broke. It was growing dark, and the wind rose. A putrid stink, as of rotting fish, assaulted me so suddenly, I was nearly sick. Something barked— not like a dog—the sound terminating in a low vicious growl.

I held my breath as I paused to listen. The sound came from the sea side of a granite ridge. Cautiously I stole closer. The cry came again, loud and sustained. Mindful that the storm might break any moment, I scaled the ridge and peered down to the rocks below.

I nearly fell off the ridge. A giant glowing monster, impossibly large, straddled the coastline, the two halves of its dazzling bulk distributed between shore and water, joined by a squirming cluster of luminous ropes. Lightning crackled. It was not one but two monstrosities, bound together by taut, luminous cables, one creature a roaring, muscular mound at the edge of the tide, the other rising like a conning tower from the sea. I shut my eyes against a blaze of lightning, then strained to see. A colossal thing with tentacles had its great coils wound around some tremendous land animal. Stretched across the tide, the coils vibrated with tension.

Thunder shook the boulders and rattled across the island. Burst after burst of light lit the rocks below. I caught a glimpse of lamplike eyes rising from the tide. The cables shook with the thunder.

I wondered why the one monster did not let go or the other prevail or be pulled into the sea. I had a sudden quick view of the land creature as it rose to scream back at the storm.

Thunder blew the night apart as a wall of water dropped from the sky. In the time it took me to scramble down the boulders and race to the cabin, I was completely drenched.

When I returned to the beach the next morning, there was no trace of anything. It was a squid, I believe, and a bear.

CHAPTER 5

My Companions

ood was low and the water rising. For countless mornings I watched the shoreline creep up till the waves now crested half their former distance from the cabin. I had given up the notion of gathering wood for a bonfire. People would be too busy rebuilding their lives to worry about stragglers marooned on cliff tops. I would have to rescue myself. It was evening now as I sat in the cabin, mulling over a plan to build a boat from the rough timbers of that floating platform. On the verge of falling asleep, I heard those sounds again, *click...click...click*. Without thinking, I threw open the door.

Looking up at me with dead, sightless eyes was a human head. I went reeling back. They covered the forest floor—a glowing sea of human heads floating just above the ground.

One came through the door. In the light it ceased to glow, and ceased to be a head. I saw its legs. It was a crab.

By lantern light its distended convex shell was a dull green with nondescript mottled markings. It was only in darkness that the phosphorescence converted these into eyes, mouth, and teeth, so that the shell glowed like a corpse's head. The thing was a crab, nothing more.

That night I had a dream. I was piloting the platform through a sea of immense waves, steering by a tiller as long as a tree. The platform barely felt the waves but drifted quickly along, broad and stable.

I was at work early, bearing tools and my preliminary designs. My first task was to detach one of the end pieces, which would go to form the framework for my boat. I worked fruitlessly for a half hour, till an idea took shape. Here, I thought, is a ready-made craft, steady and seaworthy. If it is fifty times the size it ought to be, so is the sea. Why pull it apart to make a boat that will probably not ride half so well?

I began by hammering some boards together into a great box to serve as a shelter and storage compartment. A mere lean-to at first, with patient work it became a house in miniature, snug and tightly built. Little by little I was able to detach planks from a neighboring cabin, float them to the raft, nail and screw them to the wooden deck.

The tiller was the biggest problem. To be effective it had to be long enough to control the raft, yet pliant enough to be withdrawn in shallow water. I solved the problem by assembling it in hinged sections controlled by a crank-operated crane. By rotating the handle I could raise the tiller almost out of the water. I thought, too, of rigging a mast with patchwork sails culled from sewn blankets, but abandoned the project when I realized the labor involved.

Day after day I worked at my task, my diet consisting exclusively of fish I caught in order to save the remainder of my canned goods to stow aboard the raft. I never considered eating the crabs.

There were more of them every day. Shy by day, it was only by night, when they began to glow, that they took on their terrible appearance. They had learned to climb. I saw them in the trees sometimes, clustering by dozens. Sometimes they gathered just outside my window, so that I had to drive them away to be able to sleep.

They scurried everywhere. I took to carrying a stick to sweep them gently from my path. I waded no more to the platform but poled along in a little flatboat I knocked together to bring goods from the island to the raft. I even managed to transport a wood-burning stove.

At last the raft was finished. The days were short and cold. I carefully stowed aboard everything I could think of that might be useful.

On my last day on the island I stood at sunset upon the high bluff overlooking the eastern horizon. The setting sun at my back threw red light on the waves below. Somewhere out there in the flooded world must be more land and people, I thought, along with the danger of drowning or dying of thirst and exposure. I thought, too, of those terrible fins standing out like black sails. Here I had been safe and even comfortable.

As I mused, I noticed an object floating on the red waves. It was vaguely spherical and metallic-looking and glinted yellow in the dying sunlight. Whatever it was, the current was bringing it closer.

I walked down to the beach, squinting against the sunlight on the water. Then, for the first time in—how long?—I began to laugh. Involuntary laughter shook me, and I collapsed doubled to the ground, hugging my knees, roaring till my sides ached. For the object drifting toward me was nothing less prosaic than an old Volkswagen bug. It was bright yellow and coming closer all the time.

"I'd always heard they were waterproof!" I howled to no one. And my joke set me reeling once more.

It was turning with the current, drifting away from the island. Suddenly I stopped laughing. Someone was inside.

I kicked my shoes off and plunged into the water, waded for a bit, picked my way through the drowned trees, and swam frenziedly.

It had ceased to move, as though awaiting me, impeded, perhaps, by submerged treetops. A silhouette showed through the clouded windows. Tangled in branches, the car rocked gently back and forth. The silhouette nodded too.

Gingerly I paddled over, an indefinable dread spreading in me. Through the clouded windows I could see someone in the driver's seat, gently bobbing with the waves. I hoisted myself up by the door handle. The car lurched with my added weight, but I held on and pressed my head to the opaque glass.

Inches from my eyes, a head bumped against the windshield. The hair was yellow above the skull—the dress yellow, too, like the car. A seat belt bound it all together. I drew back. My motion rocked the car. The thing inside struck the windshield with its head. I screamed as I leapt backward into the water. For I heard my name. I swear I heard my name! The car gave a violent twist, dislodged, and floated free.

I plowed wildly through the water till I hit the beach, then scrambled up the bluff and into the forest. The dense foliage did not admit the sunlight remaining in the sky but was afire with eerie light, every branch in every tree infested by crabs that glowed like jack-o'-lanterns. When I collapsed exhausted upon a high hill just out of the forest, I turned to look back at the darkening sea. Ignited by the last spark of daylight, a yellow speck drifted slowly northward.

CHAPTER 6

The Fish

t was the next day, and everything was aboard. Not much was left of my island. The water was so high, I had little fear of colliding with submerged boulders or trees.

I said goodbye to the cabin and the crabs and tried not to think overmuch of what my superheated imagination had attributed to the thing inside the yellow Volkswagen. I nodded to the memory of the squid and bear as I unfastened the lines and started to pole the raft toward the current. A slight swell assisting me, the raft made pretty good progress, edging closer to the turbulence that marked the current's edge. When the island was fifty feet or so behind, the raft entered the current, dipped slightly, then righted itself and scudded along, smartly responsive to the tiller.

I spent all day cruising eastward on the sunlit sea, toward what I hoped was land and people, the weather continuing pleasantly warm with a gentle, cooling breeze.

The night was dazzling, the moon so bright that I sat on deck reading Stoddard *On the Steam Engine,* because it was the only book I had found on the island besides unreadable best-sellers. My back propped against the raft house, I savored every piston and pressure valve till I could read no more and crawled into my bunk inside the cabin.

I awoke gently as from a delightful dream, while the earliest sunlight played over long, rolling swells. The ocean was lovely, the breeze fresh, my book engrossing, and life a vacation.

Thus I journeyed for days, drifting ever eastward, reading and rereading my book, feasting sumptuously off my canned goods, casting the empty cans overboard to the teeming silver fish keeping pace with us. Once or twice I felt the raft vibrate as if some preposterously large thing brushed against the undersurface.

Now and then I used the tiller to avoid enormous basaltic columns rising hundreds of feet above the sea. I had to begin my turn the instant I saw one on the horizon, but the raft always responded in time. I had hoped the formations were a precursor of land, but they ceased after a while, and I drifted once more on wide and empty waters.

Strange lights flickered in the night sky, resolving themselves into eerily twisting fluorescent wraiths. Water spouts, too, I saw by day, rising to colossal pillars, but always far off in the endless waste of the world.

One morning I saw a sail, erect and silver in the sunlight. I rushed to the forward edge of the raft, shouting and waving my arms. Someone seemed to hear me, for the sail quickly tacked about with a speed I would have thought impossible for a wind-driven craft. The sunlight dazzled my eyes as I cheered the oncoming sail. Then I saw it was a protruding fin streaking toward me, an enormous silver fin growing larger every second till it rose as big as a building, then suddenly plunged below and disappeared.

The creature would sheer off as soon as it smelled wood instead of flesh. It wouldn't attack the raft. Even now it must be pursuing its subaqueous way half a league beyond. Unthinkable, that it would attack the raft. I reached to open the cabin door.

Something enormous launched itself out of the water, hitting the deck with an impact that sent the raft tilting and spinning. Only my grasping the cabin door kept me from sliding overboard. It had all the wonder of another world, a monstrous silver fish, appalling, with the towering eyes and cavernous mouth of creatures from the darkest depths.

But its eye was alive with intelligence; its eye held me powerless, suspended, while the enormity writhed toward me on pectoral fins like tree trunks, till I had nothing to look at but its unrelenting eye. The eye bore right through my brain, down to the spine, insistently, entreatingly, as if urging me to some critical action now that I had it on the raft. To speak. To act. Something. Anything. I hesitated. With a sort of snort, the monster arched its body and leapt away, hitting the sea with a concussion that sent the raft once more tilting in the rocking waves. I held on to the all-but-perpendicular deck till I could stand again. Then, still shaking, I ran quickly to peer down through water the color of green bottle glass. Far below, a vast shadow swam out of sight between enormous buildings.

The action of the monster had propelled the raft out of the current into a new direction. Though I strained at the tiller till my strength broke, I could not regain my heading. I was captive now to a different and stronger current. I surrendered the tiller when I saw that the new current was carrying me straight toward land.

CHAPTER 7

Bell

The current swept me into a deep, clear channel between two mountaintops, massive and thickly forested, the higher peak more splendid, its snowcapped crest lost to sight beneath a cloud, yet I could discover no discernible landing on that side, the water ending at sheer rock. The lower peak being accessible by a broad shelving beach, I shoved the tiller accordingly. The raft eventually came to rest, and I stepped onto the shore, mooring the lines to a boulder. Once more I rejoiced in the scent of pine.

The slanting sun highlighted dancing dust motes as I hiked beneath the trees. The ground sloped upward. Insects hummed. Overhead, a hawk screamed in the sky. It was very warm. House-sized boulders splotched with brown lichen loomed around me. Brown lizards scampered at my feet.

The ascent grew steeper. Breathing heavily now, I dug my feet into the soft brown dirt beneath layers of pine needles, my head pounding with the exertion.

Insects attacked my eyes and ears until I grew maddened with the constant slapping and scratching. My way was all forest and dryness and crazy drone of insects and throbbing in my head. And always there were more boulders to climb over.

I came upon a path. It was no more than a foot wide, but it was solid, hard-packed, and swept clean of pine needles. All paths, I reflected, lead somewhere, so I confidently followed this one as it wound among hot, dry brush, descended through a miniature forest of manzanita, then rose again, to a wilderness of pines, while high across the channel the snowcapped peak contrasted with the heat all about me. The ground became level, my pace regular and even. Thick branches muted the hot sun. The air was fragrant with pine sap. I even minded the insects less.

From somewhere ahead came the unmistakable sound of water rushing over a pebbled bed. I moved through reeds and over patches of green moss, faster, until the path emerged into sunlight, and I found myself at the edge of a wide stream. In a moment I was flat on the bank, drinking in very cold water.

"Cleans inside and out!" a voice boomed behind me.

I whipped my head around.

Standing over me was a burly big man with close-cropped hair and the pugnacious jaws of a bulldog. A red cotton shirt and faded dungarees covered his muscular frame. He must have been in his sixties. He carried a cane.

"I said, water cleanses the whole being, but it is better for washing than drinking." He prodded the pine needles with the end of his cane. "Do you drink beer?"

I nodded dazedly as I rose from the stream and searched for words.

The big man clapped me on the shoulder.

"Yonder lies my home"—he gestured—"and bread and cheese and beer and ten pounds of choice cavendish tobacco." His voice was a hearty croak, fierce with energy.

Without a word I followed him as he stumped over wide, flat stones leading across the stream and on through a stand of pines to a spacious cabin fenced by a garden of red-and-gold wildflowers.

"Seem to wink at you, don't they?" my guide boomed. "Come in."

I found myself seated in an overstuffed armchair and handed a foaming mug of beer.

"Your health!" the man grunted.

"You are the first person I have talked to," I faltered. "I've too much to say."

"Then let your words speak for you. Ha! I am Bell. Hiram Bell. I own this cabin. Are you hungry?"

"My name is Paul Sant," I laughed. "And, yes, I am very hungry."

"Sant." He studied my face. "It is a good name. It is a cognate of sanctity."

In a few minutes he was scrambling eggs atop an old-fashioned wood stove, while fish baked inside. We drank more beer as we ate.

"Where sharks now swim was a village," Bell said between bites. "I labored there, but I lived here, thousands of feet above everything else. When the Wave came, it separated among the peaks, sparing mine and the big snow-covered one. Talk, Sant, tell me your version of the inundation; I have told you mine."

I talked of my adventures.

"Like Mandeville," croaked Bell, looking very much like a prize-fighter, "you eternally seek the sunrise. Did I tell you my mountain formerly held a lake on its shoulder, which, like every other body of water lower than the clouds, has since yielded its debt to ocean?"

I looked up from my beer.

"What happened to the world?"

He reached into a desk drawer and withdrew a massive briar pipe and a worn leather pouch. Courteously offering me another pipe from the drawer, which I courteously refused, he spoke while he filled his pipe, tamping the tobacco as if punctuating his sentences.

"What happened? Why, the ocean reared up on its hind legs as it was bound to do. So much was locked in reserve, frozen north and south in colossal refrigerators. Maybe it was an earthquake. Maybe this old planet shifted on its axis. Maybe the whole blessed continent just sank. Does it really matter?"

"Matter?" I said. "All the people—"

"Yes, many must have died, as we will sooner or later."

"Civilization?" I asked.

"It wasn't really civil, was it? Do you miss it?"

I made a movement as to speak, but he continued.

"Things don't last." He brought his cane down on the wooden floor. "Everything ends. We've had our Bach, our Socrates, our Saint Francis. They did their part to keep us sane and wholesome. Do you miss your childhood?"

I took another sip of beer.

"What I am saying," he said, "is that once we had much, and we made what we could of it, but now it is passed. Do you mourn the passing of civilization? I do not. We do not live for civilization. We live to build our souls up to be good enough for God. More beer?"

I was silent as he refilled my glass.

"Suppose life a five-act play," he resumed, "one of those Jacobean ones that you don't know if it's a comedy or a tragedy till the last scene is played. Well, some act has just concluded—I don't know which one. Maybe another is about to begin.

"Where we are was a mountain. Now it is an island. I live here and fish, smoke my tobacco, and drink my beer. The beer will give out, then the tobacco. I shall not miss them. See the bottle on the mantelpiece? It is Imperial Tokay, given me by a duchess. When I have drunk it, I shall not mourn the empty bottle. So with all good things. While we have them, they are a consolation and a delight. Afterwards we drink stream water."

He paused to relight his pipe. "Have you noticed that time is aberrant?"

"I tried to estimate the days since the Wave. I couldn't do it," I said.

He shook his head. "At first I marked a calendar, till the action seemed so futile that I threw the silly thing away." He swallowed a large mouthful and wiped his lips. "Things rarely operate in isolation. We have experienced catastrophic physical change; be prepared for metaphysical change. Your silver raft mate is an instance of what I mean—or your head-crabs. Anticipate more of the same. Expect to see sights stranger than you've imagined. You look tired.

"That sofa is plush and soft; you'll find pillows and blankets at the bottom of my linen press here. Go to sleep now. I am going in to say my prayers and smoke more of this blessed tobacco. Good night."

And I was once more alone with my thoughts. Civilization, I'd been telling myself, lay somewhere ahead. England, perhaps, or France or Norway remained intact; it was only a matter of going there. Bell believed otherwise. Civilization was gone, he said. Civilization was dead. But he could not know.

Yet the more I considered Bell's words, the greater peace I felt, not because he thought civilization ended, but because he, too, did not grieve for lives lost. I was not the only one to have such feelings. There was even a peculiar exhilaration now in considering a fresh, new world. True, I had found the loneliness sometimes oppressive, but I had a companion now, a fierce big man who looked like a prizefighter and brandished a cane and spoke learnedly if oddly about things.

He could not know that civilization was gone. Civilization must be somewhere. But I felt conviction only in the softness of the sofa and the warmth of the blanket.

It was dawn, and a cool mountain breeze blew the curtains in from the half-opened window. A cock crowed somewhere. From the depths of the house a croaky voice declaimed a dubious song about pirates and dainty ladies with questionable morals. The bulldog head popped into the room.

"We've a snug breakfast," Bell chortled. "Poached trout, egg steak, and braised potato. Come eat awhile."

The kitchen was well windowed to receive the morning light. Half a hundred pictures of cats garnished the pine walls.

"Last night I told you I don't miss things," Bell said, ladling eggs. "The point was overstated. I miss cats. I miss cats and fiddles and a priest to say Mass. And I miss books. Most of mine comprised the public library down where the village was. Well, I still have my bottle of Imperial Tokay." He ran a prizefighter's fist over his spiky hair.

"Has it occurred to you, Sant, that, one by one, the good things are taken from us—as though temporarily on loan to a museum? Taken and packed and shipped off—awaiting us in heaven, one hopes. I refer to little things mostly, certain amenities and courtesies. Little by little they peel off, and we see them no more. In time we even affect to despise them and speak in stage whispers of how progressive we have become. But the day sings to us; let us survey the estate."

We spent the morning roaming the acreage that Bell called his garden, festive with wildflowers but mostly given to potatoes. In the afternoon we fished the stream for trout, then hiked till dark about the island. And all the time we talked.

I could not say enough. We must have talked eighteen hours, if hours could still be reckoned; for though the days and nights were more or less predictable, the smaller units came and went on a schedule of their own.

I mentioned my academic expectations, now of course frustrated. Bell talked of books, women, and politics—and all manner of things but himself. Regardless of the subject, when Bell spoke, he argued with the ferocity of one going into combat.

So time passed in a succession of conversation and camaraderie. I helped him spade soil, plant potatoes, weed his garden; we harvested, fished, made repairs, and always we talked.

One afternoon we lounged together by the trout stream. Our talk had been of strange things—the head-crabs, the bear straining against the squid, the silver fish that leapt upon the raft. Through a breach in the trees surrounding us we could see the sun sparkling off a patch of ocean. Bell cleared his throat.

"I will tell you a true ghost story," said the familiar hoarse voice. "There was a moon, and I was tramping through ancient Semitic hills littered with fragments of broken civilizations. I had taken a shortcut across the hills because I needed to get back quickly to Cairo, to help a friend; if I did not arrive in time, something unfortunate would befall him. I knew I could reach Cairo in time to help my friend if I did not tarry overmuch. Except for a few shepherds I had seen no one in a hundred miles. The night was so still that I would have welcomed any companionship except that of brigands. It was very cold. There was only the bright cold moonlight, the thin piercing wind, the silence, and of course the eternal potsherds and bits of masonry strewn across the plain.

"As I made my way along, a wail froze the night. I stopped, my skin tingling with more than the cold. Just ahead was a pile of white, shaped blocks, disturbingly reminiscent of a tomb. And this was the source of the sound.

"The wailing ceased suddenly. Being naturally curious, I went to investigate. The tomb, or whatever it was, was a jumble of stone rent by a wide crack. I bent to listen, because something down there seemed to be whispering.

"I had a piece of candle and, shielding it from the wind, managed to light the wick, my hands shaking so much they could barely hold the candle. I peered through the crack down into a chamber. In that chamber was an unwrapped mummy, a female, standing upright a few feet below me. The mummy stood next to a bronze door fretted with some cryptic seal.

"The whispering continued. Behind that door, it said, was Pharaoh's treasure, carried out of Egypt and dropped here by the wandering children of Moses. I wondered if it were so. Go see, the whisper droned on. Gold. The loot of the pharaohs. Chills ran up and down my back, but everything inside me screamed to descend and open that door.

"I did not. I had to help my friend in Cairo. I did not have the time. I gave one more look at the mummy before blowing out the candle and backing away from the tomb. In the flickering candle-light the mummy looked as fierce and ancient as evil itself, with an expression that suggested she knew much more than I did. I jumped away from those ruins and ran farther into the desert. When I was halfway up the next hill, the whisper began again, but I was in no mood to listen. The whisper persisted. I walked briskly now, thinking of Cairo. The whisper followed me through the hills. Just when I thought it would never end, it turned into a final shrill wail. "Hiram Bell," the desert screamed. "Our time will come!" I was lighter on my feet then, and I ran most of the night, till I fell in with some camel drivers. It was only when I was back in Cairo riding the crowded streetcars that I felt reassured. I was not too late to help my friend.

"I was young then. I would do the whole thing differently now. If I met that witch mummy today, I would bless her."

"Bless her?"

"You would be amazed at the amount of damage a really savage blessing can accomplish."

"But what was behind the door?"

"Something locked in by those who knew their business. I'm glad I didn't let it out."

"But the mummy," I said. "What was her part in all this?"

"I don't know her part," he said.

It was dark now except for a fragment of moon halfway up the sky.

"I've read a lot of encounters with the so-called supernatural," I said. "No one takes them seriously."

"No," he said, "no one takes them seriously. The world is full of foreshadowings, of adumbrations and premonitions, of ghostly haunts and visitations—but no one takes them seriously. They're all pressed down, veneered, overlaid by the little lightbulbs and broad paved highways and wires that talk and tell people that existence is the accumulation of artificial lights and concrete highways and wires tingling with electricity. And people believe and feel safe and live sterile lives and lose the ability to think beyond man-made trash. But a big wave comes that washes away all the paved roads and shatters all the lightbulbs, and the wires are silent, and the people are drowned. And the veneer dissolves like paste, and all the ghostly underpinnings rise to the surface, and you can't dispel them with bright lights, because you haven't got any; and you can't outrun them on your highways, because the highways are under water; and you can't talk them away with copper wires, because the electricity is gone.

"Soon you realize that the old-fashioned eerie beliefs are the real things, and all our boastful contrivances so much rubbish, and that you and everyone else have been hiding behind them, not so much because of the ghouls and the ghosts and the whole entourage of the twilight, but because you have been most terribly afraid of God.

"Hear me, that precious wave of ours has scoured this planet clean to the lithosphere, rinsing away all the drift and drabble and nasty little headachy things that drive men mad. No more income tax, inflation, and nagging uncertainties. No more lawyers, social workers, and corporate executives. Hereafter people will live in a big way.

"Somewhere out there," he said, pointing to the sun sparkling on the sea, "is the romance and adventure of a clean new world. You, Sant Sanctus, have a place in it. Perhaps I have a place in it also. But beware of the witch mummy and her kind, because as sure as apes and apples, they have a place in it too."

I thought about Bell's new world all the next day, as we gardened and fished and as I gorged upon his few books and drank his beer. I thought about the high mountain walls, the trout-filled streams, the garden of vegetables, and the companionship of civilized thought and society. I thought of his wonderful house, the coziness of chairs and drapes and a stone fireplace, and wondered what more Earth had to offer than two men on an island.

I sat alone on the veranda that night, while inside, Bell slouched over my steam-engine book, turning the pages by candlelight. Then I looked up at the sky. The moon wore a corona, a triple circle of bright neon fog. I gazed far out over the water. The ocean looked ghostly in the moonlight. I could see only emptiness. More than ever I was conscious of great perils and the small likelihood of finding any remnant of civilization. I contemplated Hiram Bell poring over my book. Here was companionship and goodness and wisdom. Here I could read and talk and be happy after a fashion. All this I set against the fact that I hungered for civilization.

I walked indoors to Bell bent over his table.

"I am leaving," I said.

He looked up. "On to Ithaca, where Penelope weaves her eternal tapestry."

"Want to come along?"

His eyes seemed to glow for a moment. Then he reached for his cane, and the light died.

"Had the offer arisen in my more limber days, I would have danced my pride aboard the decks of galleons. Now, alas, I can only plod. No, Sant, the adventure is over for me. When shall you go?"

"I'd better make certain my raft is still seaworthy. Tomorrow I can do that, and outfit it too, providing you can spare me some provisions."

"Enough to outfit Xenophon and his ten thousand!" He laughed. "Or nearly.

"Wait." He stepped over to a closet, pulled open the door, and reached to retrieve something. "Here," he said, turning. "This is yours now." He plumped it on the table. "I hope it fits."

What lay on the table was a first-rate canvas knapsack.

"Tomorrow we'll load the raft," said Bell, pouring out two mugs of beer.

"Tomorrow," I echoed. We clinked glasses.

The next morning, when we hiked to the beach where I had moored my raft, the raft was gone.

"I meant to inspect that raft of yours," Bell said. "It reminded me of something. But it is too late now. Come, there is yet some island to explore."

We walked back, past the rambling cabin, down to a cove on the far side of the island, where I had never been. A wooden shed stood half submerged in lapping water.

"I told you there was a lake on this mountain," he said. "I used to sail it in a trim craft that once had known the sea. I moored my craft in a boathouse by the lake. Only just before that flood of ours,

I had a small falling out with the man who owned the boathouse, so I had the boat canted high and dry to yonder shed. I did not know the water would follow." He waded in and threw open the door.

Floating jauntily in the half-flooded shed was a twenty-six-foot sloop.

"There is no fuel for its engine, but the sails still hold wind. Take it, Sant. It is yare and it is yours."

We pulled down a good part of the shed before we could float the sloop into the sunlight, then tied her off and packed her with provisions. It was just such a craft as I used to sail in my college days.

I thought that night of Bell's goodness and wisdom, his sane and solitary life, and his generosity, as I tucked my steam-engine book—the only valuable I could offer—into the cupboard that housed the rest of his library.

Bell was nowhere to be seen when I awoke the next day, but he appeared shortly after.

"You needed a pocket knife," he said. "I had an extra one, and stowed it aboard along with a few incidentals. Hark ye, breakfast calls, a breakfast for heroes. Hear the warlike chant of the potatoes."

After breakfast we walked down to the sea.

"Beware the sirens' song," Bell said, shaking my hand.

"Sure you don't want to come along?"

His eyes sparkled.

"Ho! What a pair we would make stumping about enchanted isles, cutlasses drawn!" The strange light glittered in his eyes. "Alas, I would only hinder. The epic is yours; the rest of my story is falling action."

"Don't be too sure."

He smiled. "You are right. I may yet claim some adventure in your odyssey." He shook my hand again.

"I've always thought the *Odyssey* was about someone trying to get home," I said as I climbed aboard.

"Ah, weren't we all—always, even before the flood? God bless you, old Sant." Bell cast off the line. "Go and fell a cyclops."

In a minute or two I was skimming across a rollicking surge and he waving furiously from the shoreline. I must have been beyond his sight, lost in the dazzle and glare of the morning sea, as I turned back once more to contemplate his lonely figure, still waving from the shore. I had my hands full trying to keep the bow straight while tacking toward the wind, so it wasn't until some time later, after I was bouncing easily in the current, that I had a chance to tie off and hunt for lunch. Then it was I discovered that Bell had given me his bottle of Imperial Tokay.

CHAPTER 8

At Sea Again

The boat sailed cleanly into the current —the wind at one with the flow—and I splashed, headlong and bouncing, through the sunlit, sparkling sea. All morning the boat scudded through dancing whitecaps, and all afternoon through scattering spray that provoked me to laugh for very delight. At night I lay to and felt the current move me. So it was all smooth sailing that day and the next, the breeze bracing, the sea a dancing river.

The wind died the third day. One moment we charged along with breaking sail; the next moment the sail dwindled like a tired ghost. I tried tacking about, but the wind was spent, so I drifted along, propelled by the current, till after a while even the current seemed to die. Sooner or later the wind will rise, I said—with which consolation I ate my dinner and went to sleep.

The morning was overcast. The boat scarcely moved. After a

scratch breakfast I made an attempt to hoist the sail, but it dangled from the mast.

The air grew uncomfortably humid as the afternoon wore on. Phantoms of fog drifted by. The boat seemed poised upon the lifeless waters. Fog piled up, layer by layer, till I sweated from every pore, my sweat mingling with the enervating, ectoplasmic vapor. A hidden sun diffused a sickly light.

Night brought a blackness so complete that for a horrible instant I thought I was blind. Clumsily I groped for a match, almost shouting at the tiny spurt of flame.

What it illumined was the one thing beside human companionship that could ease the oppression. A present from a duchess, I reflected, toasting Bell with the black, dusty bottle. That night I drank Imperial Tokay inside the sweating cloud on an unknown sea.

I awoke with a headache and a throat parched for water, my saturated clothes clinging to my shivering body. The fog shone slightly pale, and I guessed it was day. There was no sensation of sight, sound, or movement in the white world around me.

There was little to do after I put on dry clothes and ate something. I thought all day of the things the Wave had brought, and of Bell, and of what I saw in the Volkswagen. And I thought of the thoughts I used to have when I thought the Earth predictable. After a great while night came again. But there was no more wine.

So the days passed, in a succession of gray silences and black silences. When the fog finally opened, it was in a dream. I dreamt we struck some large object in the mist, the impact nearly knocking me overboard. Immediately the boat eased off some points, while I rose to make compensations with the tiller. Suddenly the fog lifted. Bumping against the bulkhead was that yellow Volkswagen riding high out of the water. The fog fell like a curtain as I awoke shrieking in the night.

The sound of water swirled about me. The boat was moving fast.

A frenzied current sent us scraping past a vast volcanic fragment looming out of mist. Obscure shapes leapt to sheer walls directly ahead, then parted suddenly as I swept through cleft after cleft momentarily revealed in the fog. A tongue of red fire flickered somewhere ahead. I plied the tiller by instinct, feeling the current, yet I was neither swamped nor stove asunder as the berserk current drove me breakneck through white gloom and volcanic waste, the red fire fluttering ahead like a flag.

After an endless time I must have given up and slept, for I awoke, and it was night again, and the boat had come to rest in a shallow cove between slabs of lava. I could see only because of the intermittent flare smoldering somewhere in the fog.

I made a hasty meal, then crammed my knapsack full of provisions and strapped it to my back. I also filled two small canteens from the water butt and slung them over my shoulder. I tied the bowline to a rock, though I doubted I should return. If the land should prove another island, how could my boat sail against the ferocious current that brought me here?

What matters it, said I, as long as there are people? Just beyond the fog may be men and women, with food and books and the abundance of civilization. Boats, fog, deadly currents—what matters anything if there are people? I said goodbye to the boat and walked through veiling mist along the lava flow.

I made my way across a flooring of solid slabs, wet and treacherous. Sometimes my foot slipped, and I barely saved myself from a fall. After a while walking became easier as the ground turned to a layer of fine stones. Once my path was blocked by a sheer volcanic drift, but I felt along until I came to a break in the lava. The floor never rose, remaining at sea level.

As I trod this wasteland, the fitful, smoldering glow I followed flared up now and then as if given fuel, and for some seconds I saw a world harshly mineral, a twilight landscape of fire, rock, water, and ash. Then the light failed, the fog closed in, and my vision narrowed to a few yards in every direction, till the fire blazed again.

Now, as I groped inland, water swept from behind, covering my ankles and racing beyond. The tide was coming in, sweeping over the plain. In some places the water glowed with luminous algae, its bright green contrasting with the black ash and volcanic flare. The ground rose, and I left the water behind.

I continued along the plain till I was stopped by a solid wall looming in the mist. I reached out to touch cold iron—riveted boiler plates, caked with rust, like the keel of a great ship, suggesting that the land I trod was sea bottom newly risen. I felt my way along, thinking to walk around the ship or whatever it was. The wall did not end; I traveled in and out of niches and protuberances, seeking a passageway, but all I met were baffling shapes of metal, till suddenly I knew the wall was not the hulk of a single ship but a ponderous accumulation of nautical debris. Through the thinning fog I glimpsed entire ships heaped upon one another, broken decks, bulks of riven metal—a colossus of whole hulls and keels, some planted bow first vertically in the lava.

I stumbled through a gap in the wall and found myself inside an enclosure, black and clammy with fog and incalculably vast, for everywhere I heard echoing sounds of water dripping from high up. Without warning, brilliant green fire exploded all around me.

A luminous tide swept in, smoldering green, revealing tremendous metal caverns. A second wave knocked me into the blazing flood, and I emerged covered with green fire, half blinded with the light before I was able to hoist myself onto an overhanging girder.

All about me were caverns of metal spreading far beyond vision, tier upon tier, expanding chamber after chamber—a labyrinth of rooms and galleries rising to dizzying heights—assembled out of ships' parts, recognizable or dimly guessed.

The iron corridors whispered with each new tide, awaking queer echoes to the wash of the gathering waters. Rapidly the surf filled the passageways, drowning my exit in frothy fire till all was alight with green. High above, the vaulted ceiling of polished brass, arched and groined like some impossible cathedral, caught the reflected splendors.

As the sea continued to rise, I found footholds to clamber up the rusted iron walls, and reached a sort of crow's nest high above the glowing tide, bridged by a massive sea-encrusted girder, to a platform across the blazing sea. Everywhere one looked, metallic vistas opened in the endless profusion of an architect's fever dream.

What architect? My thoughts raced as I paused to draw breath before attempting the bridge. What architect designing what structure and for what purpose?

Scarcely daring to look down, I inched along the girder, high above the splash and the echoes, my only light the flood of green fire. Incalculable complexity unfolded about me with each new infusion of green. Who would or even could build such a thing?

I stood up when I reached the platform. In the reflected light of the splashing tide I could see a region below, dark and dry, separated from the water by yet more tons of ship wreckage. It might be a way out.

Still the corridors whispered each time the tide swept through and the chambers erupted a blazing green. The whispering followed me as I made my way down, guiding me, it seemed, from rafter to rafter, across partitions, over broken walls, from one handhold to another, down, ever down, till I stood on bare stone once more. I seemed more asleep than awake. Some water must have seeped even to this dry place, for pale gleams from residual foam dimly lit the passageway.

Who built the iron caverns? the whispering went.

It is a marvel, I said, following the glowing foam. But the purpose of it. The purpose of it?

For burial, came an answer.

What arcane burial demands such a monument? I asked. This was underwater. Things swam here. Things crept here. What could be buried here?

Something wonderful, the whisper went, the iron caves its monument, begun in the primeval of the world, with wooden ships that rotted, then followed by a donation of iron. Behold the door let into the pavement at your feet. Beyond the door in the heart of the caverns is the reason for the caverns. The mystery lies just beyond the door.

It lay flush with the floor, lit by piles of glowing foam, a great stone with a ring standing out from its center. A pattern seemed to burn from its surface.

See the emblem on the great stone slab. It promises wonders. Put your hands through the brass ring in its center. Pull the slab out of the floor. This is your way out. It is the answer to everything.

All the answers behind a single door. Yet something was buried here. I started to continue down the corridor.

Don't you want to know what lives beyond the door? Hurry, the light is dying. The little animals that burn the water green are dying. There is light beyond the door. I think you should open it.

All the answers? I asked, stopping.

Yes. All the answers.

I grabbed the brass ring, tugged the stone slab clear of the floor, and let it drop to the side. The reverberation of the falling slab rang through the corridors.

Something blew up. I was on my back, clasping my ears against echoes, while my body retched with the stench of rotting fish.

A white glow issued from the hole at my feet. I rose to see. Inside, something sizzled. A dot of burning brightness flung out filaments; incandescent, it crackled and sputtered and spewed, uncoiling ribbons of blinding fire till I covered my eyes just as the white flared into darkness.

I staggered back as something scrambled out. It ran screaming down the passageway. And I ran, too, along a different corridor. Through the pale-green patches of residual foam I raced, sometimes stumbling, sometimes pausing to feel my way steadily up in the great halls of iron. All was dry and dark, because the tide was out, and I blundered my way through that maze of crusted metal till I saw a red glare shining in an opening, and shortly afterwards I emerged.

I had little thought except for the empty crypt beneath a forgotten ocean. What had I loosed into the world?

CHAPTER 9

What the Volcano Told Me

y boots crunched heavily among the ashes as I wandered from the sea and farther into the night world of black and red—the volcanic stone black beneath my feet, blacker still the weird rock formations looming from the fog, black also the cinders piled in grotesque heaps, the very air burdened with black ash; while high above, the oppressive flame stained all the fog a brilliant blood red.

Convulsions, as of dynamite, tore apart the silence, followed by staccato reports like rapid gunfire. Steam rose from every crack in the baking lava. The air was stifling; the ground scalded my boots. I headed due east, toward the red blaze, the scatter, I now saw, of a black cinder cone launching red fire into the heavens. There was no other path and nothing visible beyond the radiant cone and the rising heat. If anyone lived on this land, it had to be past the volcano.

I fell back shrieking with pain when a tower of steam erupted in my path, and had to make a wide circuit to resume my way. There was greater peril. As I drew closer to the volcano, the fog brightened suddenly with overpowering heat, and I had only seconds to outrun an incandescent lava stream rolling out of the fog.

The danger did not matter, or the heat, or anything but getting past the volcano filling the sky like the great Wave that drowned the world. Only past the volcano could I continue my search for life and civilization.

After a great while of walking, I reached a point where my path skirted the volcano's base. The appalling cone faced me like a black mountain. I raised my hands against the heat and glare; there was no more water, no more air, only earth and the fire that cracked the nostrils, choked the throat with cinders. The ground shook as the volcano roared. I ignored the shaking ground, captivated by the tumult from the cone, riveted as by an oracle. The earth slipped from under me. I tried to get away then, but the erupting volcano threw me on my back. The cinder cone cracked open; a wall of liquid rock fell like water from a burst dam, cresting to a red wave toward where I lay fallen. I rose quickly, plowing through drifts of ashes, dodging cinders, as once more the volcano spoke; this time I shielded my ears from the thunder of words too great for mortal understanding. I ran till I had no more breath in my body, then gathered wind, and did not stop again till all the fires lay behind me, mere red patches in the thinning fog.

It may have been days or only hours before I used my canteen water to wash the cinders away, then bedded down on a great plateau, to sleep the sleep of the exhausted. The air felt cooler about me. It was afternoon when I awoke; the fog was gone altogether. The volcanic rock ended abruptly. Before me the entire world was one enormous mud flat.

CHAPTER 10

The Mud Flat

 retreating ocean had left behind a drab mud flat relentless to the horizon, where a shadow seemed to hover. Shadow or not, at least it was something to head for. There was no place else to go.

I stepped off the edge of rock and entered the mud. It was worse than walking through deep snow. Each step I took plunged me nearly to the knees. If the water table had been higher, I could have swum; if lower, I could have walked. As it was, I plodded along, apprehensive of sinking through mud as bottomless as the sea.

With each step I extracted one leg, planted it, pulled the other free, and took a step forward. My footing seemed firm enough. I could manage while the sunlight and my strength lasted, providing I did not drown in mud. But what about the night? I could miss the shadow and trudge till I sank down for sheer bone-weariness and became part of the mud.

For answer, the moon rose. The cursed fog; it made one forget such a thing as moonlight. The shadow I pursued looked more solid in the brightening moonlight, more like a formation arising from the mud.

So I continued through the night, lost in my thoughts, the formation growing ever larger till it loomed like a fortress in the frosted moonlight. And what was beyond the fortress? I asked the mud and the moon and the stars.

Then I slipped, plunging into soft ooze. In blind panic I lowered my head and tried to swim. It took me several seconds to realize that I could; for the mud had thinned to mostly water. And towering in the moonlight like the battlements of a castle, the fortress rose above me, a natural stone formation of gigantic mounds and boulders. It was with a feeling of wild, primitive triumph that I increased the power of my strokes till I pulled myself clear of the mud onto a great flat rock, and climbed to a peak far above the brown plain and into a V-shaped cleft, and there I eased my body down and slept.

I awoke to a morning cloudy and cold. I wandered among the crags and nearly fell into a great pool of water that had accumulated in a natural fissure. The water was fresh. I drank plentifully and filled my canteens, then jumped in bodily and did not emerge till the mud was gone. Only then did I sit down to finish the last of my food. Finally, I got up to look about me, stretched, and climbed to the highest battlement to survey what lay ahead.

The entire horizon was an ocean of sucking mud, littered with single stones and by enormous clusters like the one I occupied. The stones were so plentiful, I might not have to wade through the mud.

Gingerly I went down and began to pick my way. The mud made queer washing sounds as it lapped between the stones with a sluggish tidal motion. At least I was above the mud instead of in it. That meant everything.

Now and then I came upon a fish, stiff and arched, decaying in the brown ooze, and wondered, if hunger gnawed deep enough, whether I could bring myself to eat such a thing. After a while the stones gave way to larger clusters, and I used my hands to help me scale their steep, irregular sides. Each was the same, twenty to thirty yards across and littered with a profusion of sea rubbish—bones of large fish and pieces of hard shell and masses of dried seaweed, as well as fragments of an unidentifiable sort, covered with circular scales. As I reached the end of each cluster, I descended once more to pick my way among the mud and stones.

By sunset I was thirsty and tired, and looking upon yet another conglomeration of towering rock. "One more," I said, "and no farther; I shall rest there till moonrise and go on."

Wearily I plodded on and gained the cluster, monstrously big, its surface starred with pockets sparkling with water.

I bent down, cupped my hands, and drank till I could drink no more; then I filled my canteens, rested, and at last stood up to survey the island of stone.

As always, I found large heaps of dead sea life—with more odd fragments covered with the round black scales. Eastward, in the uncertain glare of the setting sun behind me, I could see a dark low mass on the far horizon, perhaps true land.

I was pleased with myself now that my thirst was satisfied, even comfortable after a fashion. "Today I have drunk," I told the stars flamboyantly; "tomorrow perhaps I dine."

With the sun gone, the night grew very cold, and a wind was rising from the east. Choosing a deep, dry cleft to lie down in, I wrapped myself in my jacket and was soon asleep.

I awoke hungry. Filling my stomach with fresh water allayed the pangs slightly. I tried nibbling a bit of seaweed, but it was tough and vile-tasting, and I spat it out.

After one quick glance around my islet, I descended to the stones and mud. The dense mass on the horizon beckoned. I had eaten nothing for two days.

All morning I pursued the phantom land, yet by noon it seemed no closer. I rested often now. My mind rested, too, even as my body continued across the stones. It was only gradually that my mind awakened to the fact that the mud between the stones had thickened to hard dry dirt.

I made rapid progress now that I could walk on firm ground. No longer a mark on the horizon, the great mass opened around me into a succession of low mounds and shallow valleys, sparsely covered with waving brown grasses. Here, too, I found the inevitable refuse heaps.

It was while I was crossing a broad, low valley that I came across the remains of a marine animal in a deep ditch among dry weeds. It must have been four feet long and was covered with round black scales. It was badly decayed, but its head, I saw, came to a peak, and I could make out protruding jaws with sharp teeth. The body resembled a frog's, with powerful arms and legs terminating in webbed hands and in feet tipped with claws. At once the mystery of the anomalous fragments was solved. Whatever this creature was, it must have wandered far from the sea and fallen into the ditch and been unable to get out.

I left it and continued across the valley. The hunger was gone now, and I felt only giddiness. The blood in my head seemed to beat against my inner ear. When I emerged from the valley, I saw that what I had heard was not my own blood but the crashing of the sea.

It glittered at me, deep and green and sparkling, as I came upon a white, sandy beach strewn with driftwood and scores of coconuts. It took me some moments to remember that coconuts are good to eat. And with a reserve of strength I did not know I possessed, I set about crushing their wooden shells by the simple expedient of hefting large rocks and letting them drop.

The more coconut meat I ate, the hungrier I became. It was a good while before my stomach permitted me to lie down and rest in the warm, white sand.

CHAPTER 11

One Sleepless Night

 woke to find the ocean a clamor of froth, churning like suds in a washing machine. I lay a few feet from the shoreline, the warm white sand my bed and blankets; I yawned lazily, mildly absorbed in this new phenomenon. Whatever agitated the sea began to vibrate the sand, the cliffs at my back, the very air I breathed, expanding in volume and power till the ground shook.

I jumped to my feet just before the sea erupted. Blinded by the spray, I felt my way up the cliffs, the ground snarling like an engine. When I stood far above the confusion, I took breath and looked back.

The sea was a cauldron. Incoming waves stopped short of the coast, changed direction, raced parallel to the land. I ran higher up the cliff as the raging sea hurled volleys of fist-sized rocks that shattered around me. I rested only when I gained the highest point, a projecting ridge that jutted far over the cataclysm below.

The cliff trembled as I witnessed the creation of an enormous whirlpool. I peered with amazement through the spinning funnel all the way down to a formation of black stone honeycombed with caverns. The funnel of revolving water—it looked like polished black marble—continued to widen, revealing more submarine caverns, which drained onto an acre or so of exposed sea bottom, shining peacefully now in the sunlight. It was lovely, an idyll of soft sand and fairy-tale caverns, a place to contemplate in fancy.

Everything gave way as the ocean crashed in from all sides, drowning the cliffs and caverns in a wash of boiling foam. When the big waves subsided, the sea once more lapped at the shore, with no sign that a whirlpool had ever been.

A cold wind came up with the setting of the sun, so I hunted for shelter among the crags and fissures of the hills. As I picked my way along, I made a discovery. A thin stream of fresh water dribbled from a cliff side, forming a pool that sparkled faintly on the ground. Nearby, a shallow crevice afforded shelter from the wind. I made several journeys down to the beach to fill my knapsack with driftwood and stranded fish, carrying all back up to the crevice, where I spent an agreeable evening, roasting my dinner in front of a crackling fire.

The next morning I set out to explore my new territory. For all I knew, it might have been a continent full of people, or at least an island habited by someone. I tramped most of the day around hills, over tidal flats, through marshes, and in and out of box canyons. It was neither new continent nor separate island, but only a sort of promontory arising from the dry end of the plain of mud. There were no people or animals, not even a lizard. I returned to my campsite among the hills overlooking the sea. Next morning, close by my pool, I set about constructing a shelter from the abundance of rocks the sea had spewed forth, a stone house built out of the crevice and roofed with driftwood. I worked steadily and by late afternoon had the beginning of four straight walls, and the outline of the entrance, a crawl hole in lieu of a door. The masterpiece was to be a stone fireplace flanked by two narrow windows for ventilation.

I would have worked till it was too dark to see, but I broke away when I heard the first tentative grinding of the whirlpool. I raced to the projecting point to observe the phenomenon more closely.

The cliffs uncovered by the whirlpool evidently formed part of a vast volcanic formation that extended eastward, its farthest visible extremity a single finger of stone rising like a tower on the horizon. I gazed down spellbound at the caverns draining in the sunlight, until the funnel collapsed into a welter of wash and foam.

It took weeks to complete my stone house. I found I lacked timber for a wooden roof, so used what sticks I had as shoring for a stone one. For the same reason, I had to settle for one window instead of two. Fuel, however, was abundant; the seaweed burned for hours with a hot, fitful flame. In order to conserve my few matches, I kept a perpetual fire on the hearth, replenishing the fuel several times a day. A compressed mound of seaweed stood beside the fireplace, while a higher stack lay heaped up just outside the entrance, a simple crawl hole.

I discovered the architectural shortcomings of my little stone house when the rains came; it leaked in two dozen places. In the interlude between storms, I spent some days applying additional layers from an extrusion newly uncovered by an earth slip in one of the box canyons. This was a deposit of flat, cement-colored tiles, faulted into straight-edged narrow pieces, almost like shingles. By the time I finished, that house was solid. I kept a good supply of these shingles piled outside but never had occasion to build the house up any further.

Small green plants appeared two days after the first rain. Within a week they covered the island; succulent and sweet-smelling, they soon sprouted flowers, bright electric blue, and the island became a painted glory. Then came the insects, absurd coleoptera, orange and red, with clumsy wings and preposterous potbellies, that buzzed about and were always crashing into things.

One morning I awoke to the sound of grating cries overhead, and crawled out of my house to see the sky filled with gulls, flashing like leaves in the wind, dipping and circling and skimming the ocean for tiny silver fish, which they devoured in midair.

In a few days the land grew shaggy with seaweed nests. The birds were so tame, I could pet them. They took flight at first when the whirlpool started up at sundown; but they eventually accepted the interruption, placidly ignoring the thunder that shook the land to its foundation. Sometimes the whirlpool cast up great crabs; these I baked along with the coconuts and fish in the large Dutch oven I built into the fireplace. Life seemed full.

The next invasion came by night. A ponderous army of immense sea turtles secured a beachhead among the tidal flats. To think that men had actually killed for food these megalithic boxes of primal mystery. The notion was as repulsive as frying a sphinx.

The birds must have brought more seeds, for the flowering blue carpet was enriched by something that sprouted chrome-yellow and purple flowers that dazzled the eye when the wind blew them together.

Life was no longer lonely, or hungry; I had flowers and edible plants bursting from the thin soil. And I had the seagulls. But most of all I loved the tortoises.

One day, as I was gathering salt plants on the flat marshes out of reach of the whirlpool, I met a host of barking, sluglike shapes; the sea lions had arrived. I did my best to make friends, but they shied away, and I resolved to return another time.

I was busy some weeks trying to farm my salt plants into a sort of kitchen garden, which would, I hoped, sustain me during those periods when I felt too lazy to catch or cook anything.

My task completed, one morning I decided to visit the seals. I loved and respected the tortoises but found them too contemplative for play. But a seal is like a dog that is half fish, because it has chased so many sticks flung into the waves.

When I reached the marshlands, I saw a terrible sight. The seals were gone except a dozen gnawed and grisly carcasses. About them the mud was patterned with wide webbed footprints. That was all. The day was risen with a slight chill wind, and the sun stood red and cold in an overcast sky. The sluggish waves lapped gently over the mud bank.

All day I paced the promontory, my spirits low. Those wide, splayed footprints reminded me of something I had seen or thought of.

After the whirlpool fell that night, I heaped the fire high and remembered. My first day here—when I wandered the brown sedge, nearly delirious with hunger and fatigue—I came across a decayed thing inside a weed-choked crevice. It was too spoiled to resemble much of anything, but it had webbed feet and horrible rows of teeth like a nest of knives bristling from its rotting head. I fed the fire higher.

After a while of vainly courting sleep, I put my jacket on and wriggled out the crawl hole. The full moon scoured everything to a bleached white. On the beach below, big crabs scurried; two great turtles slowly bumped among the piles of sea refuse. Farther out to sea, the waves suggested a stream of ghosts as they dashed to froth upon the moon-scoured sand.

Something moved in that water besides waves. Amid the echoing lights in every crest and trough, the ocean teemed with forms. Something out there was making for shore. Nearer it came, dividing as it hit the beach. Out of the water now, and standing erect. Nearly twenty of them. Manlike in stance, their heads rising to high peaked cowls. Spreading along the beach, they fell furiously upon the tortoises, razor-tipped, webbed claws reaching after the withdrawn heads.

Had I a weapon, I could have saved the tortoises, but I had nothing but a pocket knife. I watched in horror and disgust, yet could not suppress a cheer when I saw a tortoise bite the hand off one of the monsters. And I saw the others turn upon their wounded companion and devour it as it screamed. I cannot write the rest.

The moon had not traveled very far by the time they returned to the sea. The beach showed no movement in the stark glare of the declining moon. Shivering with cold and dampness, I returned to pass the remainder of the night sleepless by the fire.

CHAPTER 12

The Sanctuary

he sun rose red and dull, as though bleary-eyed from dissipation. The day was gloomy. A thin, piercing wind bit into me as I hiked down to the beach. I looked carefully about. The sand swarmed with crabs and sea birds nibbling at empty tortoise shells.

I needed a weapon. I could not guess if the monsters were strictly nocturnal, or if they would attack a full-grown man. It was best to have a weapon. There were rocks everywhere—perhaps one for a tomahawk, if I could find a hefty piece of driftwood.

Then I saw the shoal of fish stranded in a tide pool by last night's high tide. It was a gift not to be ignored, but the water was draining; some were beginning to spoil. I returned to the stone house for my knapsack, then hurried back to the tide pool, where I gathered as many as I could. I bore them back up the hill and deposited them in my "icebox," a water-filled trough near the window. I made two more trips, then realized I was getting low on seaweed, so hurried to another part of the beach and began to build a stack.

Even the physical labor of gathering and tying the seaweed into manageable bundles failed to dispel the sick feeling whenever I thought of the awful slaughter I had witnessed the night before on the beach. I had always accepted predators as part of the natural order of things. But these peak-headed horrors inspired me with hatred. I named them gugs, after the monsters in a story I read.

I hefted the bundles onto my back and hiked back to the stone house, dropping them just outside the crawl hole. Pushing my knapsack before me, I crawled in on my hands and knees.

Something was bent over the icebox, scooping fish into its wide grinning mouth. It saw me.

It ripped the knapsack apart as I fell on my back and pulled myself out, kicking the bundles of seaweed into the entrance, mashing them down with my boots. I poured in stones from my pile, hefting till I thought my back would break with the strain. The mound was high and heavy. Shaking all over, I stopped to listen.

It hissed at me from the window, thrusting first its pointed head, then its arm out the opening. I lifted a stone. Before I could heave it, the window was empty again. I heard claws scraping at stone. I had not made the tomahawk. I had nothing to defend myself but stones.

Below, the beach looked calm, the waves gently lapping at the white sand. Somewhere must be materials for a weapon. Ah, but would they let me? Cautiously, I made my way down, suspicious of every sand hill, and walked along the shore in quest of driftwood.

Instead of driftwood, I found a treasure. In one of the canyons that the sea periodically flooded lay the remains of a dinghy, too far gone to repair but a repository of nails and lumber. What wood remained was solid. I could make a door for my stone house if I chose to. I managed to detach a substantial beam. I could not make a tomahawk. The ropes of seaweed I used for tying seaweed bundles were inadequate to bind a stone to the wood. But with patient work, using Bell's pocket knife and an abrasive boulder, I ground the beam down to a skull-cracking cudgel.

The sun was low when I returned to the stone house. All seemed as I had left it, the boulders still piled high over the entrance. Everything was quiet. I tried to see in through the tiny window, but the interior was dark except for the flicker of a few dim coals.

My cudgel at my side, I began to uncover the entrance, removing one stone at a time, pausing every moment to listen. Nothing stirred, so I worked until I pulled out the last stone and only shredded seaweed remained between us. Through the gaps the expiring coals glowed faintly from the fireplace at the far end.

"Come out, you devil!" I thrust the cudgel into the entrance. It met with no resistance.

I took a breath and leapt inside.

A dark shape stood poised against the wall. The cudgel thundered on its head. The blow accomplished nothing: the creature was as dead and dry as the walls around us. It had been kept too long from the sea. The heat from the fire must have helped. I threw a lump of seaweed onto the coals.

The leaping flame disclosed an animal with a peaked cranium like the forbidding cowl of some grand inquisitor, along with the adroit musculature of a batrachian. Concentric rings of bulging skin circled the dead black eyes; below the eyes protruded a sort of snout filled with pointed teeth. One could make out rudimentary nostrils on the muzzle, as well as wide, distended gills on the sides of its head. Its limbs were amazingly strong for their elasticity, cartilage rather than bone, terminating in three-inch claws, and both head and body were covered with round black scales. The creature was nearly five feet tall and smelled like dead fish.

I dragged it outside, despite the loathing I felt to touch it. The carcass was astonishingly light, though this might have been due to desiccation. The monster looked even more shocking in the sunlight.

When I had seen enough, I carried it to the overhang and cast it into the water, just as the earth began to groan with the advent of the whirlpool. The body disappeared inside the funnel.

That night I temporarily sealed the entrance on the inside, using a thick, flat rock braced with my cudgel; tomorrow I would build a proper door from the wood of the dinghy. If anything came padding about the stone house, I was unaware of it. Just before I went to sleep, I named my stone house The Sanctuary.

CHAPTER 13

The Man
in the Skiff

 found more tortoise shells on the beach
the next morning, and the sand
stamped with webbed prints, some two
hands wide. I had to save the tortoises—perhaps with a stockade.
I had to do something. But first there was seaweed to gather; always
seaweed to keep the fire going. Just off shore lay a gigantic heap. I
laid the cudgel down and waded in to gather up the weed.

A peaked cowl rose out of the tide. I sprang back in the shallow
water and gained the shore, the gug just behind. Another gug stood
where I'd parked my cudgel. I broke for the cliff and dared not
look back till I was partway up the hill.

Three of them, in squatting, hopping leaps, were bounding up
the cliff a few yards behind me.

I tore up the path, expecting any moment to feel the searing pain
of teeth or claws on my back. I reached The Sanctuary, ignoring
my exploding lungs, made it through the crawl hole and propped

my flat rock in place, then collapsed for breath to keep from fainting. When I could breathe again, I removed the stone and crawled out.

Where were the three gugs? I looked down to the beach.

A thin man in spectacles, a man wearing a straw hat, blue jeans, and a bright green shirt, was headed into shore on a flat-bottomed skiff.

I waved my arms and shouted.

He stopped rowing, saw me, and waved back, then took up his oars once more, making for the beach. I forgot everything else as I started down to meet him, almost tumbling to my death in my breakneck effort to get to the sand. By the time my feet hit the beach, the man was nearly landed. He was a mere ten yards from shore when three black shapes launched themselves on board. Their weight turned the skiff over, and he tumbled into the sea. There was no further movement except that the empty skiff, having turned completely over, peacefully drifted away.

I stood long on the sand. I did nothing, said nothing, not even to the sea, which broke in scalloped ripples at my feet. I stood and said nothing. How few people there were. Bell and I, and the man in the skiff. Three of us. And the gugs had killed one. A few yards away, my cudgel lay in the sand. I hefted it, hoping the gugs would return.

But the sea remained quiet, and in this quietness I formed my plan. I had intended to use the lumber and nails of the stranded dinghy to build a door for The Sanctuary. I had a better use for them now. The very box canyon where the dinghy lay beached had high, perpendicular walls and a narrow neck toward the sea. It was one of the canyons that flooded during high tide.

I went down to survey it and measure its narrow neck, and tried to figure out how to mount a sliding gate. I had lumber enough.

The nails were rusty but intact. My cudgel was a serviceable hammer.

The greatest obstacles were the sheer, unclimbable canyon walls and my lack of tools. There was no access at all along the seaward side, and I could scramble up the landward side only with the greatest difficulty. Yet I needed a convenient way up, and a method also to cut a vertical track along each side of the canyon's narrow entrance, for my gate to slide down. I solved the access problem by building a rock platform. Carving the channel seemed doubtful, till I remembered the flat, limestone-like rocks I'd used to seal my stone house.

It was hard work. I had to quarry the flat rocks from one canyon, then carry them to the canyon I was working in, then stack them evenly in two columns along each side of the narrow canyon neck, in order to have a uniform groove for my sliding gate. I constantly had to raise the level of my rock platform, as well as keep it in repair. And I could not work when the tide was in. At night I wove seaweed nets to hold the bait for my trap. During all this time I never saw a gug. The tortoises returned to the beach, and all seemed normal again. Whenever the task seemed unmanageable, I remembered the man in the skiff and the empty tortoise shells and the seal carcasses.

The easy part was pounding the gate together. I used most of the wood, because I wanted that gate as solid as possible. Once the gate was in its grooved track, I lifted it a few inches, then jammed rocks beneath; then lifted it farther, adding more rocks, till, by applying gradual layers, I hoisted the gate all the way to the top, where I wedged it in place with my remaining wood. I dismantled the rock platform directly the gate was up, then finished the seaweed nets during the days I waited for the highest tide. The entire project took more strength than I thought I could muster. And all along there was no certainty that the gugs would fall into the trap—or even that they hadn't left the area.

The afternoon of the night of the highest tide, I stuffed my sea-weed nets with all the fish I had ever caught and dried and stored away. By whirlpool time the trap was cocked and baited.

That night I sat upon the cliff top of the narrow neck of the box canyon, close to the timber wedge that kept the watergate propped open. The moon blazed above me as it had the night the gugs raided the beach. Gradually the tide rose, spilling into the box can-yon. But nothing swam along with it. They will come, I said. The moon climbed, leaking its corrosive light onto the massed heaps of dried fish tied to the canyon's landward end.

Inside the canyon the waters sluiced back and forth, empty of all but the moon's searching glare. They must come, I said. The moon crawled to the top of the sky. Some fish, I saw, were nibbling at the seaweed bags that held the bait. Only fish. It was hours now. I was stiff from sitting. It was growing very late. Soon the tide would turn and the canyon drain. The gugs were gone.

If my efforts were wasted then, at least the tortoises were safe, and the seals. But for how long? The tide washed against the back wall of the canyon. Voluminous in the seaweed netting, the bait floated unmolested except for fish. All I knew was that the gugs were gone for now. In a few minutes the canyon would start to empty. The gugs must have moved on to a place of greater feeding. I rose to stretch, stared at the moon, then gazed back down upon the canyon.

The water surged with scores of high peaked heads, tearing at the bait, more entering the canyon all the time. On they came, singly and in bunches, passing beneath the poised gate over the narrow bottleneck, making for the bait at the landward end. I waited for the last of them to enter, then reached for the timber wedge. This is for the tortoises, I thought, and for the seals, and for the man in spectacles, who would have been my friend. Here is for all the vicious preying upon the unsuspecting. Then I pulled the props out. The gate slid halfway down, paused, then thudded to the bottom, sealing the canyon from the sea.

The canyon was a soup of black shapes massed against the bait. Little by little they reduced the great bags of bait to empty tatters of seaweed. As the tide fell, the creatures retreated toward the narrow canyon neck but found their way blocked by the gate. Some tried to break through; but the gate was solid, except for scores of little holes allowing the water to run out. Unable to follow the retreating tide, they heaped themselves against the gate, scrambling across one another like beetles in a jar. Some tried to crawl up the canyon's steep sides but lost their hold and fell back into the water. One made it nearly to the top. I got it with a rock. The tide left behind a hissing, squirming residue.

I stayed on the cliff until the sun came up and baked the canyon dry. Then I climbed down to count the lumps littering the canyon floor. Forty-two gugs dead and dried. So much rubbish left behind by the sea.

I retired to The Sanctuary to sleep for most of the day. At first my rest was sweet as I thought of the friendly man on the skiff. But a great sadness stole over me after a while. They're better dead, I told myself; like cancer. They'll ambush no more men in skiffs. Still the sadness grew, overwhelming me till I nearly cried aloud. The gugs had killed for food. I had killed for revenge. And that made all the difference. What was it Bell had said about the damaging power of a serious blessing? Ah, I should have blessed the gugs!

CHAPTER 14

Further Perils

slept to whirlpool time the next day, then ambled over to the tidal flats to visit the seals. Amid the barking, wriggling beasts some gray shape lay beached among the drift and seaweed. The seals dispersed when I got nearer, and I recognized the object as the skiff of the man in spectacles. It seemed intact. When I reached to turn it over, I had another surprise. It lifted easily, for it was carved of a single block of buoyant pumice. No wonder it capsized so easily. I could remedy that. It was my boat now. It was time to leave the island.

I was busy with that skiff for several days. I tore apart my watergate and built a ballast frame around the keel, weighted with a heavy rock. The skiff was stable now. I started the rough task of converting some boards into oars but stopped when I found the original oars washed up in one of the canyons.

I spent my last day tramping about and saying goodbye to my

friends the seals and tortoises, so that the day was well advanced by the time I got ready to leave. I took one last look at the stone house, tucked my cudgel in my belt, and hurried down to the sea. It was getting close to whirlpool time, and I wanted to be well beyond range when the dangerous currents came. I waved at the beach and cliffs and at a single tortoise that bumped along; then I cast off and rowed my way through the gentle green sea. I was not many yards distant when a wide, webbed hand great with claws fastened onto the bulkhead.

The ballast kept the boat upright. I brought the cudgel down sharply; what was left of the hand fell back. Peaked heads shot out of the sea; more claws fastened on. A gug was aboard. It shrieked as I broke its skull. Another up. I shattered its leg. Then they were on me. Cracking claws and limbs, I hammered them down, and furiously tried to row during the quiet seconds that followed. But they were up again—six—seven—and I lost the cudgel overboard, and I had only my oars. I struck hard, nearly capsizing the boat, and then they had the oar—then the other one, and I had only my hands.

Suddenly the water was empty.

The sea emitted popping sounds, erupting into tiny spouts and splashes. The earth trembled as the skiff was seized, pulled parallel to shore, then catapulted out to sea. I covered my ears against the cacophony of the throbbing, screaming earth, then tore my hands away to grip both sides as the skiff spun out with a momentum that took my breath away, racing round and round in an ever narrowing circle.

I shouted through the boiling wash as I peered into a vertiginous abyss of polished black marble. The skiff dipped abruptly, skirted the whirlpool's edge, and went spiraling down.

Pinned on my back, I lay looking up while a wall of gleaming marble shot by overhead. There was no water, no spray, only the radiant marble grooved and sparkling with iridescent highlights as the boat fell farther and farther down the glistening funnel. It was spellbinding and, in a strange way, restful. Round and round the ceiling spun, gleaming now like vinyl. I felt so relaxed, I could almost have slept—till something hit me so hard that I rolled over and over upon a bed of soft white sand.

I lay at the bottom of a sort of chimney, black and twisting and endlessly long, like a tornado viewed from the inside. At the very end shone a patch of blue sky and the sun.

I stood up.

It looked like a twilight canyon walled by wavering black smoke. The silence was unsettling. All around revolved the whirlpool, which I knew would collapse any moment.

There was no place to run except ahead to the caverns that pierced the great basaltic mass just inside the perimeter of whirling water, there to be drowned or dashed against the stones by the fury of the falling waves.

Still, it was a chance. Catching my breath, I ran toward the formation and did not slacken my pace until I stood at the base of its wall. Tier upon tier, it rose half as high as the whirlpool itself, a towering pile of black basalt honeycombed with caverns.

I raced through convoluted, titanic corridors, seeking entrance to one of the larger caverns. But they were too high. None was at ground level. By the time I could clamber up, the whirlpool would have collapsed.

Around a corner was an opening large enough for me. I could reach it by climbing a short series of rocks. They were slippery, and I fell twice, but I was through the entrance and standing. Still the whirlpool had not fallen. The rock floor sloped up. Once inside, there was no more vision.

Feeling my way, I moved quickly. Perhaps, just perhaps, I had found a way out. The way took me up and up. Possibly it connected with an island. Possibly I would see the sun again.

I banged my head badly and went reeling back but was instantly groping the walls, the floor, the ceiling. I felt empty space. There was a hole in the ceiling. I leapt, found handholds, and pulled myself into a higher chamber. The tunnel felt wide here, running upward and dry.

Then something crashed into my back, sending me sprawling.

It is compressed air, my dazed mind told me. The whirlpool had fallen. I was trapped in a tunnel with no outlet.

The greatest curiosity was myself. For I did not succumb to the peril of my situation but quietly felt my way along the tunnel and occupied my thoughts in forming plans.

One desperate scheme was to venture down and wait for whirlpool time and quickly seek another cavern. I might find one that led to the surface and possibly beat the whirlpool before its returning waters flooded the tunnel. Another idea was to climb down, fill my lungs, and try to swim to sunlight. In any event, down seemed the direction of safety. Upward led only to a blind tunnel.

Still I continued up, for the sake of motion, because the end of activity meant an end of courage. Sometimes the roof arched so low, I had to crawl; other times I felt the openings of adjacent passageways. After a while my way leveled off; I continued, more or less horizontally.

My mind reverted to whatever it was I had released from the crypt beneath the metal caverns. Maybe I was taking its place. The thing in the yellow Volkswagen grinned, but only for an instant, because the way got steep again.

The conviction came that I was finally and terribly alone. Another thought formed in the hateful darkness. You may not be alone. Maybe gugs live in these tunnels. You may not be here long after all.

The floor rose so sharply that the way went almost perpendicular now. Yet there were handholds. There were always handholds. Up was the wrong direction. I should have been going down. I climbed till my head hit rock.

I sat bent-kneed, in a little chamber, my back pressed against the final wall. Now I had to go down. There was no further passage up. I had to go down now, if only to challenge the fury of the waves. As I sat in that final chamber, the blackness and silence were in some measure comforting, though I did not know why. No, the silence was not absolute; there was a sort of vibration coming from the wall behind me.

I turned to feel the wall. It was flat, unbroken, smooth. I pounded it with my fist. It resounded hollowly. I rose, stepped back, and sent the bottom of my boot crashing through the wall. It was not half an inch thick. A mere shell that shattered from the force of a kick. I blinked at the glare of sunlight pouring into the chamber. I had made a window. Now I looked down. I was on a high rock. Beneath me a steep bank curved far down to a wide and empty sea.

CHAPTER 15

A Vision

 stepped through the window and out onto a ledge a hundred feet above a sluggish, gray sea. It was sunrise and the sky heavy and cold; I shivered from the bitter wind that pierced my worn clothes. Far to the west my whirlpool refuge hovered like a dark cloud. By my position I must have been atop the volcanic finger I had observed standing straight up from the sea. At close range it was less a finger than a sort of ziggurat, with shelves of broken terraces descending all the way to the water line, giving way in one spot to a tiny strip of sandy beach. The day grew colder as I started to descend.

All my food and water had been aboard the skiff, yet I felt little emotion beyond a certain curiosity about what lay ahead.

The wind blew harder. I paused in my descent to seek shelter among the rocks. Corrugated with windblown troughs, the flat sea looked like the leaden roofing of a medieval cathedral. As I shielded my face against the stinging wind, I saw something crawling up a far corner of that roof.

A black speck inched its way along the molded surface of the heavy sea. Painstakingly it worked its way toward my rock, till I could make out a fragile bark, propelled by a single rower. I resumed my descent and reached the water just as the boat landed.

A figure sat at the oars, faceless, shapeless, everything that might express humanity concealed beneath a dark-gray cloak. It raised one draped arm to motion me aboard.

I complied, saying nothing, and we shoved off. When the boat was well out to sea, the cloaked figure reached into a wicker basket and handed me a similar cloak. It was soft and blue, and it warmed my flesh from the biting wind. The rower took up the oars again, and the boat resumed its crawl across the stagnant sea. Not a word was spoken.

Flakes of snow floated gently down as we came to an empty little harbor. Several wooden huts stood in the distance, smoke rising from their chimneys. I stepped out onto the snow-covered dock. Without a word the rower raised the oars and rowed back out to sea, becoming a tiny speck, like an insect on a leaden roof.

I walked inland over the frozen ground, following a path through stands of oaks, which grew denser as the ground rose, until I stood inside a perpetual forest thick with snow, whose trees barely allowed the snow-colored sun to filter through. And still the snow fell.

Snugly warm in my cloak, I took the winding path amid twilight and snow. Three times I paused to examine the handiwork of men, for three times I encountered oaken plaques, like signposts, each mounted on a wooden stake. The first plaque bore the emblem of a sword; the second, of a book. The third plaque was disfigured, and I could not make out the design.

Three times too I met with joyous bird caroling bursting like bells as I passed each sign; yet the birds were well hidden in the foliage; only their voices leapt clear in the snow and twilight. The snow stopped falling.

The path twisted sharply past a thatched cottage. A hunchback stood in the doorway. He was short, red-bearded, and broad. He grinned when he saw me.

"Your cottage?" I asked, because I could think of no other thing to say.

He nodded eagerly, extending his arm to point ahead along the path I had been following.

"Thank you," I said.

The hunchback stood grinning and nodding till the cottage sank from sight as I rounded a curve. The forest grew darker.

A redheaded young woman cloaked all in black darted onto the path.

"How are you called?" she asked.

"I am called Sant. And you?"

The woman smiled. Shaking her head, she fled into the forest and cried in a loud voice, "Sant! He is called Sant!" until the gloom swallowed her.

The forest filled with darkness. I wandered on. Eyes lit up ahead. Something like a white deer crossed the path and was gone. The way turned again. Burning out of the darkness came a violet-eyed woman, her radiant white dress igniting her stunning face and hair of molten gold. She clutched a golden sword.

"He waits in the stone chapel," she whispered, handing me the sword and vanishing into the forest.

The path had grown so dark, I had to feel my way, till unexpectedly I broke into a sunlit clearing surrounded by shadow. Within the clearing stood a stone chapel. Nearby a fountain plashed into a moss-covered pool.

"What next?" I asked the surrounding forest.

A man in black iron stepped enormously from the shadow. Hoisting a sword in black-gauntleted hands, he advanced on me. I looked for a face amid the bulking iron, but the visor was shut. I shouted when he raised the sword high over my head. I stepped back. He came on. I retreated till I backed against the fountain and could not move more.

I had the sword the violet-eyed woman gave me. I lifted it like a shield just as the other sword came down. The shock thudded up my arms, sent my sword clashing to the pavement.

"Wait!" I shouted.

The one in black iron said nothing.

"There is no need for this," I said.

The black sword rose like a guillotine blade high above my head. I could not retreat from him, so I leapt forward, planting a leg behind his knee, and pushed hard with my open palms. The man crashed backward to a great grinding of metal. The sword flew somewhere into the darkness.

"Now we'll see who you are!" I lifted the iron helmet from the body. A half dozen large rats burst forth, leaving the armor empty. I fell back, shaking in the cold sunlight.

"He waits within," said a voice at my elbow. I turned to see the white deer trotting off into the forest.

"We'll see it through," I said to no one in particular. I retrieved my sword and strode into the chapel.

A dark young man with close-cropped hair and an ugly squint lay groaning on a stone bench, his back propped against the wall. Behind him a row of blackened heads grinned down at me, though human or animal I could not tell. He twisted in his fur-lined cloak as he rubbed invisible wounds.

"Why don't you play by the rules?" he asked testily.

"Why do rats walk in iron?" I demanded.

"It is an emblem, nothing else." His eyes pierced deeply, cynically. Then he said, "We know other days, don't we? Ha ha! We know other days."

He pointed to a flight of stone steps leading downward.

"I've got something good down there," he said with a wink. "Tell me what you think of it."

I shrugged my shoulders and descended. The passage opened to a flooded chamber, groined and pillared with stone and fitfully lit by torches let into the walls. Something swam in the darkness at the far end, and I bent low over the water to see what it was. A grinning gug head broke the surface a foot from my face.

I recoiled and suddenly found myself back in the stone chapel, the squint-eyed man frowning with disdain.

"I thought you'd *like* it," he said petulantly.

Four black-cowled figures passed silently through the room.

"Who are they?" I asked.

"You know," the other said.

I turned on my heel and walked out into the forest. The path led me to low crenellated walls jammed up against a flat harbor, which was choked with towered ships manned by wide-eyed, smiling mariners—the walls and ships and mariners' garments all of bright gold and vermilion and metallic blue. But the castellated walls were smaller than the tapestried ships, and the ships too small to accommodate the overlapping mariners, and the banners—blue, gold, and vermilion—seemed painted on the sky and sea, while the whole was frozen into a perspective that defied the senses.

I turned around to find myself once more in the stone chapel. The squint-eyed man still lounged on the stone bench, but now a great black beard reached to his chest, and his hair ran to his shoulders. There were more heads on the wall.

"You certainly took your time about it," he said with a yawn. He jerked a thumb in the direction of the steps that led to the flooded chamber. "Going down?" I walked out of the chapel.

When I emerged from the woods, I saw that the harbor that had held the ships was now silted over and the castle was gone. Where they had been was occupied now by a formidable fortress of black stone, bristling with battlements, rising tier upon tier, till they became lost in the immensity of the white winter sky.

I blinked and was back in the stone chapel. Flowing white hair crowned the lounging figure; his beard was white and nearly reached his knees.

"Three's all you get," he said without looking up.

The cowled figures surrounded me, pinioned my arms, dragged me down the stairs, one step at a time, though I fought with all I had. The black pool burned with reflected torchlight as they wrestled me over its depths. The gug hissed as it shot out of the water.

"Bless you, old gug," I whispered. The cowled figures leapt back, raising their arms before their faces as the gug dove into dark water.

I had one more glimpse upstairs. The white-haired man was weeping uncontrollably.

Then I was on the sea again, inside the wooden bark. The gray-cloaked rower spoke from behind the hood.

"None of that was real, but all of it was true."

"What does it mean?"

"Ah, that we cannot always tell."

"Look, I still wear the cloak you gave me and still carry the golden sword."

"They will fade."

"Who was the man with the close-cropped hair?"

"I was not with you. I cannot tell what you saw."

"Who are you? What were you before?"

"We do not talk of before. There is only now."

"How has the world changed so quickly?"

The rower faded as I opened my eyes to a red winter sunrise.

"The world never changes," the voice came floating back.

I shook myself like one emerging from cold water. My cloak and sword were gone. I was back on my rock with no food, no water, no supplies at all, with nothing to do except think. I sat down among the rocks to watch the sunrise and ponder the state of the world—grotesque now with animal mutations, and virtually unpeopled save by phantoms and delusions. How much of this new world was true and how much false? Or perhaps this was the way the world had always been, only now it was expressed differently. The wind was rising. True or false, what could I do? I stretched my arms out against the cold. What could I do? If I did not perish on this rock, I could only go on seeking land and people, and a theory that made sense of it all.

Even as I mused, out of the sunrise glided a trim, white cutter, sails billowing with wind.

Another vision, I said to the rocks, sea, and empty sky. One more experience to terrify or confuse. I would have none of it. Better to concentrate on finding the means to appease my hunger and warm my bones. I scanned the rock for traces of anything edible.

The cutter was sailing past. It seemed there were three people aboard. I could hear their conversation. They were real, and they were sailing past my rock.

I shouted, leaping up and waving my arms.

They must have heard me, because the boat turned and headed in. I scrambled down to them.

"Hello, on the island!" someone screamed. It was the first real voice I had heard since Bell's.

PART TWO:

The World

CHAPTER 16

Friends

 nearly swamped them—two men and a woman—as I plunged into the surf to grab the tow rope and tie off the dinghy they rowed in on after anchoring the cutter just offshore.

"Didn't expect to see anyone else again!" a thickset, gray-bearded man shouted as they bounded onto the rock. "Very happy. Very glad to make your acquaintance. Very, very, very happy." The other man was talking too. He was thin, bald, and clean-shaven, and he kept shaking my hand and wanting to know how I was. The woman was stout and round-faced, with a mass of wild red hair.

"We three have had adventures," she laughed. "Strange ones."

"I've had some too." I found I was laughing.

"We have food," the bearded one said. "Fish and, oh . . . ohh . . . wine!"

Wine.

"Is this your home?" asked the bald one. "Or are you coming with us?"

"Oh, he's coming, he's coming!" laughed the lady.

"He's coming with us," said the bearded one.

"Well, I'm glad to hear that," the bald one said.

"Where are we going?" I laughed.

"Everywhere," the lady replied. "Beyond."

"Back east," the bearded man said. "It's the fashionable direction this season!"

It was a breathless time, that morning. We laughed at everything, said everything, sometimes said nothing but talked to hear our voices and to ratify our fellowship.

The lady's name was Belle Zabala.

"The belle of the ball!" the thin, bald one proclaimed. "I'm Simon Girty."

"The name of a famous pirate," the lady retorted.

"It's only a coincidence." Mr. Girty coughed modestly.

The bearded man was Tanger Blake.

We ate our picnic meal and drank the wine. Then, having all my goods in my pockets, I joined them in the dinghy and rowed to the waiting cutter.

It was a beautiful craft, forty-one feet long and spirited as a colt. As we sliced across the sparkling waters, I talked of my adventures: of the warehouse, of the drifting, and of Bell; of the tug-of-war between the creature of the sea and what I guessed was a bear. When I told of the great silver fish on my floating platform, Belle Zabala gave a visible start, but I did not find out why till later. I mentioned, too, the fog and of what leapt from the haunted cavern of the luminous green tide, and of the gugs and the whirlpool and my long-nighted crawl up the finger of rock. I even told of my strange hallucination of the stone chapel. I did not talk of the yellow Volkswagen.

Simon Girty was next to speak.

"I wasn't in a warehouse, Paul." He rubbed his bald head. "I was in a helicopter. Outside Scranton. I'm not a professional pilot. I'm a building contractor, but my hobby is flying helicopters. Suddenly there was the Wave. It passed right under me but not by much. The radio just quit. And all the world was ocean.

"I reckoned the best plan was to make for the Catskills. But they weren't there. I cruised awhile. Saw some sights, too. Want to hear them?"

I nodded.

"Below me was a whole soup of white churning bodies, thousands just drifting in the sea. For miles. I didn't think there could be so many bodies. It was the current, I guess. You didn't see any—I saw them all. The current bunched them. Funny that I couldn't find the Catskills; they just weren't where they should be. Finally I saw something silver flashing; it turned out to be a corrugated aluminum shed right in the middle of a great flat rock standing straight out of the ocean. There was a blue pickup truck too. I buzzed the shed a couple times, but no one came to greet me when I set the copter down.

"That old aluminum shed was full of barrels of apple cider and cases of dried fruit. I drank the cider and ate dates, apricots, and persimmons while I waited for someone to rescue me. My main hope was the radio aboard the copter. But it never worked. That is, I guess the mechanism was intact; there was just no one broadcasting.

"No one ever came. I got so lonesome on that rock, I decided I'd take off again and try to make the Adirondacks, though I wasn't sure I would have enough gas to go much farther in case the Adirondacks weren't there.

"I filled the copter with fruit and cider and climbed for the sky.

I had another surprise then. The whole ocean was filled with fish the size of submarines. I swooped down for a closer look.

"They sure weren't whales; they had teeth like—I don't know what."

"I saw them," I said.

"I did too," said Belle Zabala.

"I guess they ate up all those bodies," Simon mused. "At least, I never saw the bodies again. I figure those big creatures were prehistoric animals, frozen in polar ice. When the caps melted, they began to breathe again."

"That's Simon's favorite theory," Belle said.

"Don't you figure that's what happened?" Simon appealed to me. "A lot of ancient things let loose by the explosion or the attack of sunspots or the quick shift in the Earth's axis or whatever it was that brought the Wave? That's where all the queer creatures come from—polar ice."

"It was certainly quick," said Tanger Blake.

"Of course it was," said Belle. "If everybody had warning, we could have built a giant ark."

"How did you all meet?" I asked.

"I found the Adirondacks," said Simon.

"And me," Belle said with a chuckle.

"Right on top of a big old sand hill. She was living like Crusoe, in a crazy hut she'd constructed out of boards and newspapers. Tell Paul about it, Belle."

"I'm a waitress. I was working at the Mile High Cafe. Just before dinner the walls caved in; I was under a million feet of water and getting conked by half the furniture in the place." She laughed. "I'm a big girl. I swam and kicked and thrashed till I was up and floating on a big sheet of plastic. I had some real scary adventures."

"We've all had those," Tanger Blake said. "And all the time in the world to tell them. If my thinking is correct, we're simply wallowing in time."

"Or outside time," I said.

"I thought of that too," he said. "And space isn't the same either. The way I figure it, heading east as we all were, we must have left the United States a long time ago."

"You mean we crossed the Atlantic?"

"I suspect the Atlantic doesn't exist anymore, or the Pacific, or any other sea one can put a name to. The same goes for dry land, which may exist now only as a handful of mountaintops. And even they may be sinking. I'm talking about subduction—you know, when one tectonic plate dives beneath another and gets converted back into liquid rock? Paul, the lava you saw coming out of that volcano might have been rewarmed portions of what used to be Miami or Fort Worth."

"That must be it," Simon said. "No wave has enough water in it to cover a continent. The land must have sunk. What do you think, Paul?"

"But when land sinks in one place, it generally rises somewhere else," I said.

"Unless it gets liquefied," put in Tanger.

"Do you know, Paul," Belle said, "I don't miss a thing. I don't even feel sorry for all the people."

"It's the time distortion," I said, "if Hiram Bell's theory is right. Can you feel sorry for people dead a thousand years?"

"Could it really have been that long?" Belle asked.

"It's very confusing," said Tanger. "The flood seems to have occurred many lifetimes ago. But we did not live then. Yet we're here and the world is not. Your medieval vision, Paul, may have been produced by this chronological aberration, like a breakdown of files in a computer with a bad virus. Any theories?"

"Maybe time takes a while to right itself again, like a half-capsized boat," I offered. "It may be your company, but things feel much more normal now than at any time since the Wave hit."

"That's good," Tanger said. "A half-capsized boat. I'd say Paul is right."

"I feel more real than I did six hours ago," Simon said.

"That proves it," Tanger laughed. "Six hours ago such a definite measure of time would have been unthinkable."

"Here's another thought," I said. "Everything in my medieval vision seemed as real at the time as the deck we're standing on. Yet some of the real things I saw earlier—the gugs, for example—are more like creatures found in visions. The question is, how does one determine what is real?"

"I'll tell you how," answered Belle. "If it makes you feel good when you're doing little things—working, cleaning, cooking, or fixing—it's real. Otherwise, no matter how good it looks or how pretty it smells, it's as empty as all that moonlight on the waves."

We slept then, at least three of us did. I stayed awake as long as I could to savor the reality of my companions. Nothing disturbed me now, not even the thing in the Volkswagen. I hoped they slept sweetly—Belle, Tanger, and Simon. Paul Sant would sleep sweetly, because he traveled now with friends.

CHAPTER 17

Belle's Adventures

o we sailed on, taking turns at the wheel, each of us pitching in to keep the cutter in trim and heading east. There were no more islets, just an unbroken wash of sea.

"My turn to steer, Belle," said Tanger one moonlit night. "Why not tell Paul your story?"

Belle settled herself comfortably in a deck chair.

"Paul, that fish that jumped on your raft—it was just like . . .

"No, that isn't the way to begin. Listen, Paul, I didn't move around like you. Once I hit high ground, I stayed put. Of course, it wasn't really high ground anymore, it was an island. Mine wasn't much different from other islands, I guess, except for the garden.

"I'll try to describe where I was. Pretend you're in somebody's vegetable garden, only it has fruit too. And there's an apple orchard. All this is up in the mountains, not near anything—just by itself. At one time there was a farmhouse and a barn, because I could trace the foundations poking out of the grass; the buildings must have burned down long ago. But the vegetables and fruits were still there, reseeding themselves season after season. There were apples and melons everywhere, and grapes and berries, not prime and plump—as they would have been if someone tended them all the time—but thin and wild. And all edible, wonderfully edible. Simon's fruit was dried," she laughed playfully. "Mine was fresh.

"It was lovely living in my garden but lonely and at the same time romantic in a strange way, like I had come home after all the years of counters and dishes, tips and tables.

"Simon compares me to Robinson Crusoe, but I don't think Crusoe ever made anything like my shack. What I did was take the piece of plastic that saved me, lay it on top of some big rocks, and anchor it down with smaller rocks. Then I gathered driftwood—there was a lot of it—and made front and side walls, and even a door, fastened with some pieces of rope I found. I had fresh water from a little stream. And this and the melons and the apples kept me alive.

"I had no way to make a fire. Rubbing sticks together didn't work. Not far from the shack I kept my combustion pile, which I made out of some old newspapers I found in a leather trunk by the foundations of the farmhouse. I piled some leaves on top of the papers, and some sticks, and stuck a few logs on top. Every day I rubbed sticks together, but they didn't even get warm. Still, I didn't give up.

"One particular day was hot and humid, with a lot of electricity in the air, so that my skin itched and my hair stood away from my head. I was busy with my vegetables, while the day kept getting darker and darker, and the electricity began to tickle so much, I was scratching all over. When the thunder started, I went into my shack.

"I was afraid at first of the lightning, which began to fizz like power lines shorting out. I couldn't be sure whether my plastic roof would melt or protect me if lightning struck it. As it happened, the roof was spared; but lightning struck something near by, so hard that the world went white. I smelled smoke and went out to investigate. My little pile of wood was on fire.

"I cradled those burning sticks like they were children, carrying them inside, along with all the loose wood nearby. I made a hearth, feeding the flame till it roared. It toasted me delightfully just as the storm fell like a flood on my little shack. It was a monster of a storm, but I was dry and warm, and I enjoyed the water streaming off my plastic roof.

"I don't know how long I lived in that shack, but I kept the fire going all the time I was there. The sun rose, and the nights came—I never counted them.

"This will interest you, Paul. I had one friend. A fish. He was as large as a house and shining with silver scales, like a knight in a children's story. There was a sort of pier made up of big rocks on the beach, which you could walk across and get pretty far out to sea. I usually went there when I wanted to think things over. Well, I was there one day, looking, just looking. Suddenly, an enormous silver fish burst out of the water like a submarine, drenching me all over. He was practically at my feet, so close he could eat me. I was startled but not frightened, because his eyes were like a saint's. I could have reached out and hugged him if I'd wanted. Instead we just stared at each other a long time, until he made a sound that sounded like a laugh, leaped clear out of the water toward the setting sun, and landed with a splash that drenched me again. And, do you know? The water seemed to enjoy him as much as I did. The waves rocked up and down like they were applauding. I didn't care that I got wet. I wasn't lonely anymore.

"He came to see me every day, at sunset, at the end of that stone pier. But he never splashed me again. Just for a minute or so, he would rise up and look at me with those compassionate eyes, then dive down again. I loved him.

"I had another visitor—a sort of animal. It was about three feet tall, a slight creature, with weird skinny arms and large round eyes, like a drawing a very young child might make of a man. I don't know, maybe it was a lemur. I found it prowling around the shack one afternoon. It frightened me at first. I tried to give it apples, because it looked hungry, but it wouldn't eat them.

"Sometimes it looked so human, I talked to it; I even used sign language. But it was an animal, not a man, so of course it didn't respond. Mostly it just roamed around in the dusk. I don't know where it went in the daytime, unless into a hole at the bottom of a cliff not far from the stone pier. I often saw the creature hanging around the hole, and guessed that that was its lair, though the creature may only have been looking for food.

"One night I watched it eat a fish. The front end was in its mouth, while the tail flapped back and forth. All I could see were those large round eyes fastened on me as the creature worked away at the fish, and all the while the tail flapped. I had a bad feeling, like all the things I thought I'd got away from had returned.

"I felt pain, grief, and horror, all the while that tail was flapping.

"It snowed that night, and the next, and the next. It snowed so hard, I was afraid to leave my shack. I stayed inside until the snow stopped. By then the food had run out, so I went to pluck something from my garden. But the garden was gone. Everything was buried—the garden, the orchard. I dug but found only snow. Oh, except for one hard, unripe apple. I knew that when I ate that apple, all my food would be gone. So I didn't eat it.

"Then I remembered my fish. I hadn't seen him since before the snowfall. I hadn't even thought of him. I thought of him now that I was starving.

"Over and over came the thought, it's only a fish, like a big tuna, and it would be good to eat. You must kill your fish. I seemed to taste it in my mouth. Then I realized the lemur had been looking at me all the time. It looked more like a man now than an animal. Its little hand held a long branch broken off one of the fruit trees. The end of the branch had been sharpened to a point.

"It was just before sunset that I crept down to the stone pier, the lemur beside me. Suddenly my fish was there, all gleaming in his silver scales. He swam right up to me, looking directly at me. His eyes were deep and sorrowful.

"I raised the sharpened stick. The lemur was jumping up and down like a monkey. The fish just rolled over on his back and stayed there. I was very hungry. I saw the lemur's eyes. The fish's eyes were underwater, so I couldn't see them. But I felt them.

"I drove the wood harpoon deeply into the snow. The lemur hissed and lunged at me. Without thinking, I reached for that dried apple I had in my pocket and threw it right in his face. It struck his eye, and he ran hissing across the rocks and down into his hole. Then I turned once more to my fish.

"He gave me a look that reached to parts of me I didn't know existed. And he made that same laughing noise he did on the first day; then he leapt toward the sun, high out of the water, and came down spinning like a corkscrew, drilling into the water. I watched him dive below till he was just a tiny speck of silver.

"The next thing I knew, the sun had melted the snow off all my fruits and vegetables, and I was ravenously cramming whatever I could into my mouth. I had the strangest—the best—the most wonderful feeling a human being can possibly have.

"The sun went down, and I went to bed. And still I had that feeling. It faded gradually during the night, melting into me rather than evaporating—if that makes any sense. When the sun came up again, there was Simon landing in his helicopter."

CHAPTER 18

The Narrative of Tanger Blake

ave you ever noticed," said Tanger Blake one afternoon, "that whenever we have a good thing, we spoil it?" We had been cruising steadily eastward over a calm sea.

"Take southern California, for example," he persisted. "Remember California? It was seashore, plains, and mountains, and it had the best climate on the planet. And because it was so desirable, everyone came and made it undesirable. They killed the space, the plains, and the climate."

"The last I saw of California," I said, "was when I floated over it on my surf mat."

"I floated under it," said Tanger.

"How is that?"

"On my way up to the sun. You see, Paul, I was not in a helicopter or on a mountaintop, or in a warehouse, when the Wave came. I was under the sea.

"I am—was—an engineer, working on a project we called the Base. It was nothing less ambitious than an underwater mining and processing facility planted firmly on seabottom somewhere between the West Coast and Hawaii.

"The Base was a venture involving several companies, and I believe the government had a hand in it, too. It started relatively small but was intended to expand into a sort of village, mostly under the sea. The core of the facility rested well below seabottom, while the top of it stood far above the surface, like an oil rig. Anyhow, it was in its second stage of construction when I got involved. Personnel included a building crew, a large staff of technical experts, medical people, unskilled laborers, and engineers like me. We had a team working twenty-four hours a day, and a unit to feed them. My job was to design a giant power plant to replace the temporary one we were using while we set things up; it was to be a far-reaching energy source that would eventually maintain an expanded facility.

"Most of us were topside when the Wave struck. I was luckier. Archer and Travis and I were in a miniature submarine returning from an expedition to determine whether a certain bit of underwater real estate would support the power plant I wanted to build. Archer and Travis were the pilot and navigator.

"We had no notion of any wave. All we knew is that we were spinning over the seabottom, and that the bulkhead was groaning. Archer was a good man and got things even and quieted down, and we started to surface, so that if the bulkhead gave, we would not be crunched like a tin can under a trolley. But we could not rise far, because our spinning had fouled the ballast ejection mechanism. Travis was meanwhile on the radio talking to the Base. There was confusion there. Everything topside was gone, and the flood had gone down the main shaft before they got the hatches closed. The entire top story was now beneath fathoms of water. Try to come in, was their best advice. Well, as I said, Archer was a good man, and with Travis helping him (I knowing nothing of the operation of a submarine) and me cheering them both on, we got safely inside the launching shaft and drifted up till we secured ourselves at the main dock.

"There were thirty-four men and women there. We responded at first with efficiency and bravado—said and did all the right things as we waited for rescue. When rescue didn't come, some of our engineers launched improvised snorkel towers so we wouldn't suffocate before a rescue party arrived. Rescue was on its way; it was only a matter of time, we told one another.

"But down there we had no time, no way to distinguish the days from the nights. Our clocks and watches flashed the same meaningless four zeros in a row. And that is all we knew of time. We tried to keep our courage. But much of courage depends on what comes in on the radio, and nothing came in on the radio. Still, we serviced our systems through an endless succession of meals and sleep periods, all without days or nights, without time.

"Let me try to give you a feeling of what it was like down there. First of all, we were forty fathoms deep; more, really; we began at forty fathoms, but the Wave had made sea level much higher.

"Second, as I said, the facility was not yet completed; what we had was only minimally functional. The inner bulkheads had not yet been positioned, and though the outer ones were designed to resist formidable pressure, there was a constant moisture about the walls and fixtures, reminding me of what those World War I submarines must have been like.

"Nothing really worked well. The lights, for no apparent reason, would suddenly dim, as if suffering a drain of electricity. Sometimes there were actual blackouts, which were of greater or lesser duration. The air was stale.

"Morale got very bad. Some of the men misbehaved with the women; there was jealousy. But mainly there was fear.

"I was for packing as many of us as we could inside the submarine and taking a chance on surfacing before the walls imploded, but no one would hear of it, not even Archer, and I could not do it alone. Everyone kept insisting that we had enough food and air and that eventually a rescue team would pull us out.

"I'm coming to the worst part now.

"The largest area, which was designed to be a rec room, had a big picture window that looked onto a patch of seabottom brightly illuminated by floodlights. We made this chamber our headquarters; there we discussed possibilities of escape and rescue as we watched the denizens that swam, crawled, or slithered just outside the window.

"There was a further complication. The Wave had opened a trench along the seabottom, twenty yards or so from the picture window, a long, straight gash just on the edge of vision.

"The incident occurred during a moment of argument. The discussion had been more than usually acrimonious, eliciting a great many personal remarks. I had turned away from the window for a moment to see about some coffee boiling at the other end of the chamber.

"There was a gasp. Someone shouted, 'Outside! Look at the trench!' I turned to look across the room at the window but could see only a little because of the crowd gathered at the glass. But what I saw left me shaken."

" 'What's happening?' called one, entering at that moment.

"Still the crowd obscured the window. They were making strange noises now, though I caught a few coherent words.

" 'They just cling there. Eat our souls,' said one in a pleading voice.

" 'Deformed!' shouted another. 'Deformed!'

" 'Turn off the lights!' cried someone from the back of the press. 'Please, turn off the lights. Screen, bring a screen.' The floodlights were turned off.

"The window was covered, and we fled the room.

"It was as though they had looked on Medusa. We were scientists, engineers, hard and practical. Intelligent, resourceful, intrepid. But all who had seen were changed. I, who had caught the merest glimpse, found my mind impaired. What of the many who had gazed?

"Some shambled through the metal corridors, speaking gibberish; others laughed immoderately, refusing to admit they had seen anything. The few who had seen nothing asked questions that nobody answered.

"Eventually someone sealed the rec room off with a welding torch. It made no difference. All the outer chambers were fitted with windows. We could not avoid these rooms; someone had to inspect the seals for leakage. We disconnected all the outside lights and covered all the windows with makeshift screens, but it didn't help. Whatever was outside carried its own light, like the white glow from decaying timber. Sometimes we heard screams from one of these rooms, and the bravest of us would rush in to find the screens down and the worker in a panic at what floated a few feet away in the water. With averted eyes we pulled him out.

"After a while no one did any work at all. There was eating and sleeping and a sort of ambling about. The people—women as well as men—became hateful to one another. Hardly anyone spoke anymore. I was no exception.

"The difference between them and me was that while they had settled into their existence, I wanted desperately to get out, even if getting out meant drowning. I said again and again that we ought to try to patch up the submarine, but Archer had gone—no one knew where—and no one else knew how to operate the complex controls. I would go to where the submarine was moored and try to figure out how it operated, but that was mostly guesswork. Still,

I persisted in urging my companions to escape with me, because I found it annoyed them.

"They grew furious and spitefully tried to prevent my trips to the dock, going so far as to weld shut the hatch that led to the berth where the submarine was. They took to watching me closely, too, lest I find a way to get to the submarine. Though none was willing to share the venture, they didn't want me to leave them. Now and then they locked me in my quarters, where I would have perished for lack of water and food had I not found a way to crawl through a service vent into the storage compartment of the adjacent cubicle. Sometimes they came to let me out; more often they forgot about me. I did not mind. I was glad that my presence irritated them.

"The men of the project got worse and worse. I'm afraid they killed the women. And their faces changed. Some acquired a bulging-eyed, bloated look.

"I was dozing one time when I awoke to find Travis and two other men standing over me. One had a welder's torch. Travis said they were going to cut my head off and flood the facility.

"I was quicker than they. I grabbed the torch and fled through the corridors. They were too far gone, I guess, to come after me.

"Most of the lighting was out, so I had to feel my way along the cold, moist metal. All the screens were off the windows. I met nobody, though I could see the backs of certain persons at the windows. I had the premonition that whatever was outside would be waiting for me by the submarine. I planned to close my eyes once I opened the hatch to the docking area and then grope my way into the craft and cover the large pilot window with my jacket. I forgot to close my eyes as I used the torch to cut through to the landing dock and managed to start the little submarine and move her out of the launching shaft, her sides groaning all the while with the pressure.

"But I remembered to cover the window when we got under way, for I had an uncanny sense of things clinging to the hull. Gradually we rose, till the groaning ceased, and I was high enough that incoming water would have merely drowned instead of crushing me. That is when I heard the pops, one after another, as if the lighter pressure burst the parasites clinging to the hull.

"Immediately I felt free of the mental miasma. I was amazed to find the submarine operations manual in a compartment in plain sight. I studied the manual furiously to find a way to blow the ballast when the submarine began to sink again. This is when I floated under California. Nothing worked, and I sank deeper, till the air sang with pressure and the girders began to groan again.

"Something began to bump against the bulkhead. Some external agent was nudging me up toward the surface. I peered out the window, which I had uncovered, half expecting the horrors that had driven us mad below, but whatever force was at work remained invisible to me.

"When the depth gauge told me I was considerably higher, I decided to try the ballast switch once more. This time it worked, and I rose quickly and eventually broke surface.

"The vessel floated on a wide and empty sea, but at least I had sunlight, and when the sun was gone, the stars. Fortunately there were emergency rations aboard, so I neither starved nor dehydrated. But I drifted aimlessly, because the engine ceased to work. After a while the vessel began to fill with water. It was subtle at first, a thin film, then the merest trickle, then a steady stream. I did what I could to plug the leaks, but nothing made much impact on the badly burst seams, and the submarine began to founder.

"Just as it was going down, sinking from under me, I came adrift of a tiny wooded island and swam toward the beach. Like every other bit of ground above the sea, that island was a former mountain, but a mountain that had a considerable lake on it. The lake was intact, high above the surrounding sea. Nearby, in dry dock, was the most beautiful sailing ship I ever saw.

"I lived some time on the island, thinking many things that I had not the time to think about before. After a long while I observed that the island was growing smaller, till the ocean rose to mingle with my lake. I managed to free the cutter in time to float it as the water rose around me. I had done some sailing years before, so was able to wander to another island, where, next to a grounded helicopter, I found two persons singing in the woods—Simon and Belle.

"I never learned what bumped me and my submarine up from oblivion. And my coworkers? I suppose they're still down there, what is left of them. May God be merciful to them."

"Tell Paul about the thing you saw," said Belle.

"Mind you," said Tanger, "it was only a dot I glimpsed between bodies clustered at the window."

"Tell him, Tanger."

"It looked like a burning white fabric, that's all, a burning white fabric too bright for the eye."

We were silent a long time. I took my turn at the wheel. Belle and Simon trolled fishing lines, while Tanger sat bowed in thought. After a while he seemed to shake himself.

"The question now," he said, looking at all of us, "is how do we fit into our new world? Any opinions, Paul?"

I had none.

"Belle?"

She shook her head.

"Simon?"

"It almost seems like we were spared for a purpose," Simon hazarded.

"I have that feeling also," I said.

"I am not a scientist," Tanger began. "I am only an engineer.

And you, Paul, and Belle and Simon—if I may say this—are not eminent people, not statesmen or religious leaders, the kind one would expect to found dynasties. Better people than we perished in the Wave. If we have been spared for a reason, it is not because we are somebodies; it is because we are nobodies."

"This is certainly different from the end-of-the-world books I've read," said Simon Girty. "There's always a corny love triangle."

Belle struck a pose. "Well, here are three desperate men and a gorgeous woman. Fight duels or something. Unless, of course, you would all like to marry me."

Our laughter would have sunk a smaller boat.

"I guess we're just naturally civilized," observed Simon Girty.

"There is land ahead," Belle said simply.

Shafts of sun pointed out a looming shape.

Every gust of wind carried us closer to a high landmass that grew darker in the dying light. In a while we beheld trees.

"Well," said Simon, "here is nothing that has been underwater."

"You're ignoring the kinks of time," said Tanger. "For all we know, this was mucky seabottom when Paul was vacationing in his marine warehouse."

It was deep twilight as we sailed into a narrow cove between two heavily forested arms of land, wooded to the water. We dropped anchor, boarded the dinghy, and rowed for shore.

We saw eyes sparkle like fireflies just beyond the first trees. Dozens of large animals seemed silhouetted against the black of the forest. We could make out deer, clearly—and elk, possibly moose.

"Oh," said Belle. "We're up north."

"It's too hot for north," I said.

"Another novelty of our strange new world," Tanger said. "Now we have moose in the tropics."

"Three to unload," Simon laughed as the boat bedded into the soft, shallow sand, "one to explore."

"Explore what?" I asked.

"For a campsite," said Tanger.

"Find us a good place with running water, Paulie," Belle said, "so I can take a bath."

"Very well. You three drudge away. I'm off on a hike." I made straight for the interior, losing myself in the wilderness of pine. It was nearly dark, but an early moon kept me from stumbling as I stalked through beds of pine needles, my ears alert for the sound of running water.

I found no sign of humanity; but everywhere were deer, fox, rabbit, and beaver—all just out of reach. I reveled in the sight of what Hudson Bay must have looked like before the trappers accomplished their devastation. At last I came upon a stream, clear and bracing, abundant with salmon. I had found our campsite.

I got back to the cove just as the wind began to blow.

"Tanger!" I called. "Belle! Simon!"

But all was dark, empty, and silent, save for the sighing of the wind.

The dinghy was gone. I ran farther down the beach. The cutter was gone, too. I was alone once more.

CHAPTER 19

The Wind

I t was a spooky night. The wind was howling now. To keep warm, I hiked back up the cliff and burrowed among the standing roots of an immense cedar as the forest shook around me. Now and then the wind died, and I could hear a snapping of branches, as of large animals moving through the brush. What had happened to my companions?

Perhaps the animals got them, I thought.

Perhaps nothing got them, said the wind. Perhaps they left you here to drag your days out alone, forever forgotten and unwept. I huddled closer among the roots. It was far more likely that Belle, Simon, and Tanger had suffered an animal attack. Bears, mountain lions—perhaps something worse. Whatever it was must have been terrible indeed to assault three able-bodied adults.

The wind sank to an insinuating whisper. Your companions were as real as the rower on the corrugated sea, as substantial as the squinting man in the stone chapel.

But these were different from the others.

Yes (the wind was louder), but cannot they be equally false? Perhaps it is your fate to fall from vision to vision, each time assured of reality, each time disappointed, frustrated—doubting at the last whether anything exists at all.

"These are not my thoughts!" I shouted, clutching my head in both hands. "I believe in reality."

Now the wind screamed.

Put your head inside the Volkswagen! That is all the reality you'll ever know!

All night the wind shrieked its burden of despair, I feebly resisting the confusion in my mind. Somehow I must have slept, for I awoke, bleary-eyed, in the dim half-light that precedes the dawn. Something immense was staring down at me.

It was a man on a brown horse, and both were looking at me.

"Well, this is a caution," said the man. "I say it is a caution; do you not think it is a caution?"

I had to admit it was.

"Now here you are, lifelike and breathing, *animate,* as they say; behaving for all the world like a lifelike, breathing, animate creation. It is so; do you not think it is so?"

I allowed as it was so.

"Furthermore, here I am, an equestrian. I'll bet you never thought to see the like; confess, did you ever expect to see the like?"

I conceded that I'd not expected the like.

"Well," he said, dismounting, "the first thing I reckon to do is invite you to breakfast while we discuss impossibilities."

He was a short, spare fellow in a plaid shirt, faded dungarees, and a slouch hat.

"I'll just make us a fire and cook some fish. You've no particular objection?"

He searched out a little clearing and began to lay stones in a circle.

"Now Henry and I landed yesterday, a couple of miles down island. We were getting low on provender." We both gathered dried wood and stacked it in the stone circle.

"My name is Donk Radlitt," he said.

"Paul," I said. "Paul Sant."

He extracted a sort of tinder box from his shirt pocket and ignited the wood. Then he turned to a gunnysack draped across the horse's back.

"There's fish in here. We'll need a couple of long sticks."

A few minutes later we sat down to a sumptuous hot breakfast.

"Even Henry likes fish. Here, old fella."

"I've lost my companions," I said suddenly. "Two men and a woman. We landed yesterday. I went out to reconnoiter. They stayed to set up camp. Have you seen them?"

"No, nor Henry hasn't either. But we'll try to find 'em. Let's cook more fish. Say, how'd you survive the Big Wave?"

"I was in the basement of a marine warehouse that had oxygen tanks. I swam out after the Wave passed and floated on a surf mat to an island."

"I was on a big old mountain, cooking for a construction team of a lot of other fellas. Suddenly there was a sound—it was like a wind, only it wasn't. The sky started acting funny. It got real cloudy, and something kept flashing like sheet lightning. We all waited awhile; then the whole crew of us piled into a couple of utility trucks and tried to drive down the mountain. That's when we ran into water, coming right up onto the road. That road just disappeared into water, like it ended in the middle of the ocean.

Only there wasn't an ocean there a little while before. The rest of the party was for staying till someone came to rescue us, but I was anxious to get home, so I made a raft and drifted. I saw some strange sights. You want more fish?"

"No, I'm full. Thank you."

"Just as well; there isn't any more. No matter. We can catch some. But let's start looking for your friends, and while we're at it, you tell me where you come from and where you've been and who you met and what you've been thinking all the way down from the Big Wave!"

I gathered my few belongings. I was yawning uncontrollably.

"Looks like you didn't sleep too good," my companion said.

"I had bad thoughts. Besides, how could one sleep in all that wind?"

"Wind?"

"A gale," I said.

He looked squarely at me. "There wasn't any wind where I was, and I wasn't half a mile from here. You tell me about that wind, and about those bad thoughts."

I briefly recounted the doubts that had assaulted my mind. "Like another person's thoughts," I said.

"Let us have a look at your bedroll. Sometimes a bad bedroll makes a fella not sleep well." He walked over to where he had discovered me among the cedar's roots.

"There's a big old hole here. Hold on, I see something." He jumped down between two roots and disappeared.

There was a whistle, and a moment later his head jutted from the forest floor.

"Have a look-see. Whew! No wonder you had such an unsettling time—with such a bedmate. Look down there." He climbed out of a hole I hadn't known existed, scarce two feet from where I had slept.

Tangled in the roots a few feet below was a mass of dirty human bones.

"Probably not a nice fella. What's that hat thing he's wearing?"

"It looks like a ceremonial headdress," I hazarded.

"Just the sort to give you the wrong thoughts. He was getting even with you for disturbing his sleep."

CHAPTER 20

Hudson Bay

"Just because their boat is gone doesn't mean they went with it," Donk said. "Boats can drift away, especially if you don't tie them right. We need to explore some before we start spreading ourselves all over the ocean. You see the logic of this, do you not?"

I had to agree.

He gave a hitch to his trousers. "Let's walk a bit."

It was a big territory we set out to explore, this new Hudson Bay, a land teeming with creatures. While we tramped through the forest, innumerable animals—grouse, wild turkey, small deer—seemed to gather behind every bush. We walked on, almost brushing the animals aside. I spoke of Bell, and Tanger, Simon, and the warm-hearted waitress.

"Yet," I concluded, "the fact that we are all Americans, surviving from different parts of the country, might argue that the catastrophe was only local in a sense. Perhaps the rest of the world was spared."

He stared at me blankly.

"That mountain I was on when the Wave came wasn't in the US. It was in Nepal!"

We walked till the forest opened to a broad plain.

"Hang on," Donk said. "We can ride some of the way. You can ride double, can't you?"

Henry did not mind. We left the forest and cantered over pampaslike grasslands, red deer darting from the long grasses to keep pace with us.

"I found Henry on a strip of mud flat that was just sinking into the sea," Donk turned to yell from his cockpit position on Henry's back. "He was a bit standoffish at first, but when he realized our common peril, he became as gentle as a soul could be. Now here are the three of us trotting as merrily as kitchen kin." A wilderness of game loped, scrambled, or slithered around us as we continued on.

We rode the day out. Sometimes we took turns, sometimes we rode double, and sometimes we walked, as the deer gamboled mere feet away, and mink lent their musky odor to the heady perfume of pine. When it was too dark to search further, we made camp beneath a stand of pine on a cliff a little above a lagoon.

"This is the end of our crissing," my companion said, snaking several stone-weighted fish lines out over the water, their makeshift metal hooks baited with the tiny crabs that ran persistently over the rocks. "Tomorrow we start crossing. If anyone's here, we'll find 'em."

That lagoon was an angler's orgy. In no time at all we caught a mess of fair-sized perch. We lit a fire. As we were both ravenous, there was little talk till we had finished dinner. Outside our campfire the forest shone with the eyes of deer and larger animals I could not readily put a name to.

The frying pan washed and scoured with sand, the utensils

cleaned and put away, my companion stretched out on the earth, his back propped against a tree.

"I have been thinking," he said. "Now that there are two of us, civilization may rightly begin again. We are a community, and a community thrives best with a division of labor. I'm a cook. I reckon I can make just about anything taste good that isn't too repulsive. I can fill the cooking department, but you've got to come up with something in return, on account of our being a community. Now, what can you do? Can you lay bricks or cut timber or doctor broken bones?"

"I taught English literature."

"Very well, I'll cook and you learn me lit'rature. I never had time to read much, except books about General Ulysses Simpson Grant. He's my idol. But that's history. Lit'rature is different. Mind you, I'm a good cook, and I expect good lit'rature in return." He was thoughtful a moment. "Now everyone's heard of Shakespeare; he's the best there is. Even I know that. Have you got Shakespeare on tap?"

I acknowledged I had.

"Good. Put me down for Shakespeare. Now how about Milton? I've heard about Milton, though I'm blessed if I know what he wrote. Never mind. You got Milton? Very well, mark me down for him too. That's enough for now. I reckon Shakespeare and Milton are fair payment." With which arrangement we turned in. My last impression that night was of large animals moving quietly through the forest.

Donk had the cook's calling; he could cram a trout full of leaves he picked up, roast it till it crackled, and have it tasting like something encountered at a preflood debauch in a jacket-and-tie restaurant.

In exchange for which, each day as we walked or rode along I told him something about one of Shakespeare's plays, gave the plot, quoted what I could from memory. Then we discussed the characters and anything else Donk wanted to talk about. We did *Macbeth, As You Like It, Hamlet.*

So those Shakespearean days rolled by, Donk preparing the meals while I supplied the poetry. For a change we switched to Milton. Day by day we persisted through the wilderness, arguing sin and salvation in *Paradise Lost,* taking our meals from the sea or off of branches. At no time did we consider the animals as food.

There were stoats, foxes, beaver, with a complement of bobcats, snakes, and weasels, giving way as we moved through the wilderness; the more intimidating animals—the elk, moose, and black bears—giving way, while keeping pace beyond the thicket of wild shrubbery—all the animals giving way.

As a relief from the forest, one moonless night we decided to camp along a rocky strip of beach a few yards from the trees. We had to choose our steps carefully—Donk, Henry, and I—since the way was slippery with algae and pockmarked with tidal pools; but it was good to be out of the forest and under open sky. We built our campfire in a dry hole and set up our fish to bake. Not far from us, the forest crackled with a thousand tiny sounds. As dinner conversation I told Donk about the silent rower and the occupants of the green chapel.

"The whole thing was like a medieval allegory," I concluded, scouring my plate with a handful of wet sand.

"Allegory? What's allegory?"

"It's when you use a person or an animal to stand for some inner moral quality, like courage or truth."

"Allegory," he repeated. He set down his empty plate. "It is a good word. Do you suppose someday folks will make allegories about us?"

Something screamed in the forest, a long, loud ululation.

"A wolf?" I asked. "Was that a wolf?"

Something else took up the cry. A third and a fourth.

"It's a whole pack of them," Donk said.

The howling went on. Then the howling died.

The forest was silent till something growled.

"Sounds like a lion," Donk said.

The howling erupted again, louder. Something grunted. Other things growled. The forest echoed with animal shrieks and wails.

All was suddenly quiet. The forest whispered with moving leaves, punctuated by the crack of branches. Bushes rustled as if trod upon by muffled hooves. Then, again, there were sharp cries and rumbling growls.

"I don't care for this," Donk remarked. "The forest is filling up."

"Like someone stalking," I said. "Like someone sneaking up."

"Like soldiers," Donk said, "getting ready. I think they mean business now."

"Let's get away," I said.

"It's too dark to move without breaking your leg. Let's just keep the fire hot."

We held our ground, because we had nowhere to go except the sea, and talked quietly while we waited for dawn to show us a way around the potholes. With Henry close by, we talked of life and its comforts and of those unspeakable pains that tore some lives to red rags. We talked till the forest screamed again.

We held our ears against the cacophony, Henry stamping and neighing, and waited for the attack. Explosive hoots, guttural grunts, and bestial growls assaulted us, from just beyond the circle of our campfire, but still the animals did not attack.

The noise died, and the forest began to whisper again.

"Some of those sounds were made by bears," Donk said after a while. "I saw a man once ravaged by a bear. It wasn't a large bear neither."

Something snarled. Something grunted. A wolf howled. The forest erupted again.

Donk patted Henry's neck. "There's always the ocean." We waited, for the attack or for the sunrise.

The larger ones moved in at dawn, but they did not attack. There were bears everywhere, shuffling over the sand in the new daylight, and moose stood like armored statues, forming a barrier between us and the forest, but a quiet, quiet barrier. The rising sun showed us a clear path along the strip of sand, wider than before because the tide was out.

"Let's move," Donk murmured.

Slowly we stole along the margin of beach—Donk, Paul, Henry. I looked back. The animals were keeping pace behind.

"We're being served our eviction notice." Donk chuckled. "Keep on walking, but slowly. I got it figured out now. They went for your friends because there were three of them and their human smell was stronger. I guess they took that boat after all. You were probably next on the animals' list, but you hooked up with me, and they let us both alone for a while till they could figure us out. Keep walking. They must have done for the Bone Man; he was probably a hunter. They didn't let him get away, but they'll let us."

"Why?"

"Henry," he said. "He's one of them as well as one of us. I reckon they'll let us float ourselves over to another island."

"Do you mind telling me how?"

"Why, the same way Henry and I got here, of course. We have a barge."

"A what?"

"Here, let's get on Henry. It's light enough to ride now. See over yonder, just around that little hill there."

We trotted till we reached a parting in the cliff.

"There," said Donk. "Did I not say so?"

I nearly fell off Henry's back. Riding in a brisk, windy sea was my old platform.

CHAPTER 21

Henry

 ran down to the deck and over to the boat house, Donk close behind. My stove was there, my bed, my things.

"That is the platform I told you about," I said breathlessly, "the one that carried me to Bell's island."

"Now I kind of thought it was."

"Where did you find it?"

"I will tell you, but only after we cast off. Look behind you."

The entire animal population, it seemed, was advancing on us. We untied the ropes and cast off. The current carried us foot by foot, till a highway of water separated us from the island. The animals hooted, trumpeted, bellowed, shrieked.

"I guess they'll feel more comfortable now," Donk said.

"Tell me how you came upon my platform," I said when the island and the noises had disappeared beyond the sparkle of the waves. "I left it moored at Bell's island. Then one morning it was gone. Where did you find it?"

"Sit a spell while I take the reins," he said. I propped myself congenially against the boat house. He took the tiller and began to maneuver.

"Do you remember that I told you I built a raft when I was atop that mountain in Nepal, and went sailing solo because none of the others wanted to go with me?"

"Yes."

"Well, that raft took me far across deep waters. In fact, I floated such a long time, I despaired there would ever be such a thing as land again. Finally, though, it happened. My little raft went to pieces within sight of a stretch of grassland. Well, I got my belongings onto my back and swam for shore. Then I commenced to trudge across the flattest, weediest succession of real estate a fellow can imagine. After a while I began to think the same way about the grassland as I had about the everlasting ocean, that it occupied all the world and I would be at it forever. I had well-nigh walked myself out when an idea welled up one day, formed of everything I knew about walking and weariness and grassland. That idea was a horse. But novel as the idea was, I couldn't take full credit. For off in the distance trotted something brown and equine and undeniably four-legged. I guess it was its proximity that put the notion into my head.

"It was coming my way, a beauty of a chestnut stallion. He stopped when he was pretty close, and we took a long look at each other. He didn't shy away when I tried to pet him but gave me a bite or two. You wouldn't know it now, but he was fractious. Nonetheless we stayed together in a loose sort of way.

"It seemed an ideal place for a horse. With a big old stream tearing right across the plain, Henry had all the grass to eat and all the water to drink, whereas I, except for some roots and things, had mostly the water. Henry would run off by himself sometimes in the morning, just for joy of life and to show me how independent he was. Generally I saw him at sundown, rearing up against the clouds in the most picturesque way. I wondered Henry didn't appreciate me more than he did, but there is no telling about a horse.

"Day after day I followed that stream, now and then getting lucky and pulling out a fish to eat. It was at my hungriest that I envied Henry; this was a paradise if you were a horse.

"Then one day I noticed that the water of the stream didn't taste good anymore, while the banks were losing their firmness. I figured I had blundered onto a bad, marshy bit of ground and would soon be up again, but when it only got worse, I backtracked a ways, and found that what had been firm a few mornings ago was a slough of mud.

"The notion came to me that the land was sinking, and that I'd best figure out how to preserve Henry and myself in case it disappeared altogether. It was a nice problem, as there was nothing but grass to work with. Even if I could have woven some sort of boat (which I couldn't), there was little likelihood it would sustain my weight let alone a horse's.

"After a while the land became mostly ooze, except for some bits of higher ground, where Henry took his constitutional.

"One day I smelled the sea ahead and realized I'd better come up with something quick that would float the both of us to safety. Well, I thought and I thought, while that sea smell got stronger, but I got no further than the idea of a boat made of mud, which I could maybe bake in the sun—when suddenly what do I hear but Henry's hooves thudding along something wooden.

"I plodded over to where the commotion was. What do I see but this barge beached right in the middle of all the ooze. I knew it was time to go and that Henry was invited too. Can you imagine any lesser craft you could use to carry a horse?

"He seemed reluctant to go at first, but I struck a bargain with him. 'Henry,' I said. 'Here you have prime grass and drinking water in seemingly endless supply; such richness, however, will soon vanish beneath unfriendly waves. Furthermore, despite indications to the contrary, I know you are a sensitive horse, beset by loneliness even as am I. Let us board this barge in perfect amity. It may be our fortune to discover other equine friends, preferably a she one.' Horses understand eloquence.

"He was as docile as cream after that. He even let me ride him all over that platform. I spent most of my waking hours back on the marsh gathering grass for Henry and storing it away in the boat house, and also taking in an occasional fish for myself. In a day or so the water level crept up so that we were afloat. After another day we were no longer on an island.

"I soon learned the hang of your steering apparatus, and we had a pretty easy time drifting about in search of water and fodder, and, to keep my promise, a suitable companion for Henry. But we never found anything but more empty grasslands, probably sinking like the first one. Not until we reached the place where you and the Bone Man were sharing quarters.

"Now that the final mysteries have been cleared up," he said with a grin, "what say we return to Mr. Shakespeare?"

We did *The Tempest*. When we came to Ariel and Caliban, Donk's face lit up.

"You do not have to tell me. I can see it as plainly as I saw that bone character under your cedar tree. It is simple. I remember the word. They are allegories, both of them. Do not contradict, I know it must be so."

"No," I said. "They are symbols, not allegories. Allegories exist in unreal worlds and stand for abstract qualities—like the characters Sin and Death in *Paradise Lost*. Symbols thrive in the real world, both as themselves and as a part of a higher, inexpressible reality that goes beyond the world. Look upon Ariel and Caliban as figures that embody certain elements of refinement and coarseness, and you'll see what I mean."

He scratched his head. "It is deep. I'll warrant it is deep."

"Think of Sin and Death as representing ideas we can put in words; we dress up the ideas to look like people; that is what allegory is."

"Yes."

"And think of Ariel and Caliban as standing for things we can't put in words. That is what symbolism is."

"It is deep," he repeated. "Imagine an idea walking around in a suit of skin. But in the real world nobody ever meets an allegory named Mr. Sin or Miss Death."

"No," I said. "In allegory the name spells out the whole character. Symbols require work to interpret."

"Like the tug-of-war you saw between the bear and the squid. That is a case of symbols."

"How so?" I asked.

His eyes narrowed. "Which one were you pulling for?"

"The bear."

"Precisely. Because he is furry instead of slimy and looks like things we're familiar with. But remember, the bear can kill you as dead as the squid can."

"The question is," I said, "which side are we on? The bear's or the squid's?"

"It is a poser, all right," he said. He stretched out on the deck. "Good night, Paul."

"Good night, Donk." The sea splashing against the wooden deck provided a kind of lullaby. Pictures floated down of gentle green landscapes, and I floated up to meet them.

"Returning to allegory." Donk's voice put me back on deck. "In real life you never meet anybody named Mr. Sin or Miss Death.

But what if Mr. Sin or Miss Death use an alias? Why, a fellow might shake hands with Sin and Death every day and not be aware of it."

"We need their names," I said patiently. "In allegory the name spells out the character."

"But what if they don't give their real names? What if Mr. Sin, for example, calls himself Ferguson and Miss Death is Mrs. O'Shaughnessy? Are their characters any different for the phony names?"

"They wouldn't be true allegory," I replied with a yawn.

"A snake can bite you just as dead if you call it a llama" was his conclusion. "Good night, Paul."

The gentle green landscapes floated easily down.

"Tell you one more thing." The landscapes vaporized. "All the squids and bears and symbols and allegories—piled from here to Pluto—never did as much harm as one bad person. It's people hurting other people—stealing from them, vandalizing their property, injuring them by brutal attacks, even telling them how to think and what words to say—that makes a hell on earth."

"Which brings us back to *Paradise Lost*. What a difference it would have made if they hadn't eaten that apple."

"Maybe they'll know better next time."

With which observation we both went to sleep.

The current must have taken us far. At dawn, ice-topped mountains filled the sky; beneath them a green and fertile land expanded to infinity. Even as we stared wide-eyed, the ocean's surface burst into a rainbow geyser as a giant silver fish breached the surface and plummeted down to the liquid world below.

CHAPTER 22

Grant

h, this one's prime," said Donk. "I can feel it; much primer than the last place. This one's built for people. We have a chance here.

"Got to look for a mare; got to look for sheep, cattle, dogs. For your friends, too. Later on we can set up our city. Say, what do you think we should call it? How about naming it after Henry here? We could call it Henryville."

"Let's see what's here before we think about names," I said.

"Or why not call it after General Ulysses S. Grant? It is a good name; you know it is."

From where we stood it seemed like all the earth we would ever need. We beached the platform on the soft sand of a wide shore.

"Let's have some exercise," Donk said, leaping astride Henry's back. Henry's hooves clopped across the platform; then horse and rider were on the beach and out of sight behind a cover of palm trees, while I made the platform fast to a big tree stump and followed more casually.

Everywhere were palms and white crystal sand and the sound of the ocean waves. It was a big land; the snow-clad mountains in the distance rose to a measureless turquoise sky. As I wandered high up the slope inland, I was impressed by the clearness, the brightness, the solidity of all I saw. There was something else. There was a feeling of home.

High up the bank, I encountered three streams of water draining to the ocean. Beside one of these streams, three men shoveled sand into canvas bags. Donk and Henry appeared from over a rise.

"A cowboy!" shouted one of the men.

"No," said another. "It is Sir Galahad." He pointed at me. "And he's fetched his squire along to dust his armor."

"Pay them no heed, gentlemen," said the third. "You are heartily welcome here."

Donk and Henry trotted over to join us.

They were strong, thin men in their early fifties, obviously enjoying their work, though they immediately abandoned it to lead us farther inland. The crystal sand gave way to lush emerald grass as we walked up from the sea.

The jokers were Burt and Joe; the serious one was Mac.

Just ahead lay a valley gorgeous with orange trees and surrounded by high, snowcapped peaks. Nearby stood a dozen wooden sheds and a couple of outdoor tables.

"Twenty of us live and work here," Mac said.

"What do you call this community?" Donk asked.

"We've no name for it as yet."

"How about naming it after General Ulysses Simpson Grant?" Donk said with a strange smile.

"Grant. Grant. It's a peach of a name, all right," remarked Joe.

"Never heard a better," said Burt. "Grant. I like it."

"We'll have to vote on it," Mac said. "We vote on everything," he explained. "Sit over at the picnic table. I notice Henry's already eating. Here." He handed us a platter. "You fellas help yourselves to dried fish and onions."

"Where is everybody?" I asked, my mouth full.

"Working," said Mac. "Fishing. Some are fossicking."

"How's that?" asked Donk.

Mac reached over to pour water from a pitcher that sat on the table. He handed us each a wooden cup.

"We send a few fellas out every couple of weeks to look for edible plants and other useful things. Can't spare too many, because we need the rest for work. If this is a island, it's a big 'un—maybe a whole darn continent."

"Sometimes a few of us go over to scout the smaller islands nearby," Burt said.

"That's how we found Tom," said Joe. "He was holed up in a tree house a few islands south of here. He's the one who brought us goats."

"We found Sandra on another island," Burt said. "She was just fishing all day long with a line tied to her big toe."

"Do you have a Belle Zabala and a Tanger Blake and a Simon Girty?" I asked.

They shook their heads.

"You lose these folk?" asked Mac.

I told about their disappearance from Hudson Bay.

"Sounds like Flashpool," Mac said. Joe and Burt nodded.

"How's that?" Donk asked.

"Flashpool," Mac said. "Burt gave it that name. Tell them about Flashpool, Burt."

"Well," said Burt, "it's an island that sometimes acts like a magnet drawing boats and stuff like steel shavings."

"Parts of the island are smoky and shimmery," put in Joe. "With black rocks that wave in and out like they haven't made up their mind to be real yet. You pass it along the western sea—where I reckon we all come from."

"Me and Thad and Mule came riding down that way once on a fossicking trip," said Burt, "and got caught in a current we couldn't bust out of. We didn't know then, but it wasn't a current; it was that magnet working. Well, the magnet quits just as our boat is pulled into a little harbor. I looked on shore, and when I saw all that glittering, I voted we give the island a bypass, but Thad and Mule wouldn't hear of it, they had to go explore. I stayed in the boat and watched them walk right into a pool of twinkling light.

"The next thing they did is disappear. I got out quick to look for them, only I made sure to stay on the rocks that weren't shimmering. It was no good." He spat. "They were gone."

"How awful," I said.

"Not so awful," Burt said with a grin. "I never cared for Thad and Mule."

People came from all sides to crowd around us as we finished our meal. It was a mixed group of thirteen men and seven women who lived here, mostly country folk ranging in age from mid-thirties to late fifties. Besides Burt and his brother, Joe, and Mac, there were Will and his sister, Lolly, along with their boarder Mr. Hanson, a carpenter, a large and serious Swede who, toolbox in hand, had been elevated with them to the top of the Wave, as the three toiled one day to repair the roof of their house. There were Pearl and her daughter, Opal, both singers; Minnie and her sister, Bedelia, who had kept a sweets shop; and Sandra, the mail clerk. And there were Tom, Al, and Woodrow, and Lou and his wife, Mabel. In addition there were four more men out fossicking.

"The odd thing is," Mac laughed, "none of us are farmers. I was a gas inspector; Burt and Joe were auto mechanics; Lou and Mabel had a grocery store; Tom was a bartender—if that gives you an idea. What did you do, Donkie?"

"I was a cook."

"Well, that's something. And Paul?"

"I taught school."

He whistled. "Well, that really is something."

Now we were twenty-two.

And a horse.

We went to work right away. We talked as we dug fish traps in the shallow water or scoured the forests for edible plants to transplant and cultivate. We talked as we gouged utensils from hard stones or shaped fallen timber for additional cabins. Always we sought perspective.

Each had come through the flood in a different miraculous way. Al was a plumber. He claimed to have floated here in a bathtub, but I did not believe him. Mac said Al was trout fishing from his skiff along a stream in the high country when one day, instead of following its usual course, the stream continued far down until it merged with ocean. Al lay back in the skiff, lit a cigar, and complacently drifted across the sea till eventually he drifted right into our harbor.

Lou and Mabel, when the waters lapped at their second story, loaded up all the canned goods of the grocery store they could dive for, and sailed the seas on a modified barn door. Burt and Joe shared a cabin on a high mountain. When the mountain began to float, they sat in their rocking chairs on the porch and watched the scenery go by, day by day, till their mountain came to rest, forming a stationary island within sight of where we stood. What manufactured commodities we possessed came mostly from their shed, and almost all our vegetables originally came from their garden. They even kept a few chickens, whose eggs graced our wooden platters.

The loveliest surprise to all the settlers was the orchards of peaches, oranges, and apples, bursting with fruit, awaiting them on the mainland. These orchards became the pride of a rural community with no rural experience. But everyone pitched in, pooling what agricultural skills they knew from working in their gardens.

At the close of that first day the inhabitants proudly led Donk and me to the scene of their latest agricultural enterprise. In anticipation of the great crop they would raise, the entire citizenry had cleared an acre or so of the high native grasses that covered the little valley near the settlement. Unfortunately there was not much to cultivate besides a few transplanted vegetables from Burt's garden, and some wild watercress and native onions. Nonetheless, we were assured that part of every day was devoted to enlarging the cultivated area by pulling out more weeds. Donk stooped over to gather up a wisp of weed that had failed to get stacked with the rest. Then he stared at the cleared ground.

"Nice, ain't it?" Burt said with a grin, Joe and Mac nodding behind him.

Donk Radlitt surveyed the massed pile of weeds just beyond the acre of bare brown soil. He crossed his arms.

"Hard work digging those weeds," Mac said, "but worth every drop of sweat, don't you think?"

Donk's face wrinkled.

"It's a heap of work." Joe was plainly nervous. "But now the weeds are gone, we can get down to the real work of planting something good to eat."

Donk's foot began to tap on the newly turned soil.

"You're acting strange, Donk," Mac said. "Don't you appreciate what we've done?"

"Yes," Donk said. "You have pulled out all these native grasses you have, to make room for some crops you don't have. Is that not so?"

They allowed as how it was so.

"And you've taken up all the grasses and stacked them in bunches preparatory to drying them for fuel. Is that not so?"

The citizens conceded this point.

"And you intend to burn all the grasses you dug out, and then dig out the rest of the grasses and burn those too. Is that not a fair assessment of your intentions?"

There was a general nodding of heads.

"Fortunately," said Donk Radlitt, "your mischief is not complete. I see there is still much grass left in the ground, is there not?"

"Why, we should say there is."

"Yet, as you say, given time, you would remove this also, and burn it with the rest. Is this not true?"

Again they nodded their heads.

"Why, you infernal potato heads!" Donk roared. "Those weeds you're pulling out are wheat!"

"Well," muttered Burt, "at least we'll have bread."

So I worked alongside the others, doing what I could to nourish our community, taking joy in the work and the companionship and the sense of purpose, while each day I waited for Belle, Tanger, and Simon. But they never came.

We all ate our evening meal together outside on the benches that Mr. Hanson had built in the wide space between the cabins of the little community that called itself Ulysses S. Grant. Dinner was the time for practical talk about what had been accomplished and what remained to be accomplished, but it was also the time for whatever talk anybody had desire for.

It was during one such dinner, several weeks after our arrival, that Pete and his cousin, Zachariah, returned from their fossicking expedition. Donk and I were introduced.

"What did you all get?" asked Burt.

"We got some berry bushes in Zachariah's knapsack there, and some roots that might be good to eat, only they don't taste too good unless they're biled. And we got a few flowers that will look good planted by our cabins."

"We would have got more," Zachariah said, "but we came to a place we didn't like."

"We were following a stream," Pete continued, "right down inside a avalanche of trees that piled up like midnight. The stream spreads out, the trees looked like they were reaching out to grab us, and everywhere around is the coldest, darkest, loneliest swamp you ever saw."

"Not lonely," Zachariah corrected.

"No sir," said Pete. "It was howling with gators and snakes, and things I don't even know the names of."

"We called it Black Swamp," Zachariah said.

"Because it was so dark," Pete added.

"It went on and on," said Zachariah, "black and cold."

"We were glad to leave," said Pete.

"Did you meet two men and a woman?" I asked.

"We didn't see any humans," said Pete. "Only swamp things."

"And maybe a couple of haints," put in Zachariah.

"I'm going to look for them," I said. "I'll fit a sail to my raft and explore every rock and islet between here and Hudson Bay, starting with Flashpool."

"The raft is gone, Paul," Donk said.

"Gone?"

"I guess you didn't tie it tight enough."

"Then I'll make a boat."

"You don't need to make anything," said Al, the plumber. "You are welcome to use my skiff anytime."

"Thank you, Al. I'll start right away. Burt, how do I get to Flashpool Island?"

"That's easy," Burt said. "Just go a bit back the way you came.

Of course you'll be against the current, so you'll have to row twice as hard as you did getting here, unless the magnet's working, then all you have to do is hold on. But if it ain't working, you just plow west and a little bit north and you'll see a whole bunch of islands, long, lean, and low to the ground. But you don't have to worry about finding Flashpool, because it blinks at you. And there's another landmark. Just beyond the beach on a high cliff is a rock formation that looks like a modern statue."

"A statue?"

"A modern one that you can't figure out—only it's big, twenty times bigger than life, and looking down at you like it would do you all the mischief in the world. But you're going for nothing," Burt cautioned. "You won't find your friends if they've been taken by Flashpool."

"Maybe they weren't taken," his brother offered. "Maybe they just drowned or got eaten by something."

"We'll help you find them," Mac said. "Can't spare but one man. We got our planting and our building to attend to, but we'll help you find them. There may be no need for you to go fossicking at Flashpool, though. I suspect Butcher and Tea Presser are there now."

"Who are they?" Donk asked Mac. "Paul and I should know everybody, but we haven't yet heard of any Butcher or (what do you call him?) Tea Presser."

"Butcher and Tea Presser are Australians. They took Butcher's raft, they said, to fossick around the outer islands. But after talking to Burt, they seemed awful hot to explore Flashpool. They should be back any day now."

"Unless they were taken," said Burt.

"Or torn apart by sea snails," suggested his brother.

"Which of you fellas wants to go with Paul to help hunt up his friends?" asked Mac.

Several raised their hands. But Donk raised his quicker.

CHAPTER 23

Flashpool

o once more we were afloat between islands, this time westward between Grant and Hudson Bay, in quest of Flashpool Island. Day after day, we piloted the skiff against the current, seeking the island that winked, but all we found were empty places of grass and sand.

Then, one sunrise, as we threaded a narrow channel between a maze of sandy islets, something bright flickered.

"Pull for that one," I said. "East again, into the sun."

We rowed with a will, narrowing the distance between ourselves and the bright inconstant object.

"See," I said. "It shimmers."

"It certainly has an insubstantial air," said Donk. "Here, let's us put our backs into it."

"Hurry," I said. "Hurry!"

There was no reason to hurry or even to suppose anyone was on this island. Yet I felt a kind of certitude that every stroke brought me closer to my friends. Donk seemed to catch my frenzy, for he strained at his oars as though his back would crack.

We rowed amid the shimmer into a little cove, right up to the shelving beach, directly beneath beetling black cliffs dominated by a black and cryptic pile frowning at us as we rowed sweating in the sunlight.

Donk whistled. "That's the statue, Paul. Modernistic isn't the word for it. What does it look like to you?"

"Hard to tell from here," I said.

It was like being inside a mirage. The beach was a flat expanse of gray rock, intermittently blazing into patches of incandescence, dazzling the eye, then fading again as tremulous shadows rose like heat waves from the constantly erupting patches. And all the while that other shadow, from the grotesque statue, floated waveringly over us.

We beached the skiff onto a solid-looking boulder and tied the line.

"If anyone's lost, this is the proper place to lose them in," Donk said. "What were the names of those Australians that were supposed to be here?"

"Butcher," I said. "Tea Presser."

"Likely they're lost too. Let's try something. Oh, Butcher! Oh, Tea Presser!" he called.

"Tanger! Simon! Belle!"

"I guess we'd better go look for them."

"I think I should go alone," I said.

"We aren't even sure they came to this place."

"There's a chance, Donk."

"Then, hang it; we'll both go."

"See the way the shadows beat against the gray stone like waves, and fall back when the bright patches flare? I'll wait till the shadows wash in, then go fast when they're on their way out."

"I can go as well," Donk said.

"I'll try to work my way up the cliff to the statue; from there I should be able to see a good part of the island."

"Just you be careful. Or I can go instead."

The bright waves flickered on the edges of gray rock.

"Here I go."

Ignoring the flashes and swirls of darkness, I raced toward the cliff. My feet flew over the flat beach, taking the rocks at the bottom of the cliff, propelling me into a narrow defile toward the top, the landscape exploding all around in showers of brilliance.

Yet all I felt was the cold presence of that grotesque pile lowering over me in the uncertain light as I ran up between detonating flashes. At last I made the top, collapsing onto the flat, wide summit, panting to get my wind. I looked at Donk as he sat in the skiff far below.

Then I made myself turn around to peer at the monolith above me.

"Can you see anything, Paul?" Donk's voice came floating up.

"Yes," I said. "I can see everything."

"What do you see, Paul?"

"I see the statue."

"What is it?"

"It is a gug."

There was a pause. Then "Ah. I've wondered what they look like."

"On the other side," I told him, "is a little valley, then some forest, and more hills. I don't see anything shining there. I'm going down to explore."

"Paul, some of the rocks that were waving around a little while ago are dull now. Maybe that's a good sign. Paul?"

"Oh, my goodness," I cried. "Tanger, Belle, Simon!"

"Do you see them? What do you see, Paul? What do you see?"

"I see the dinghy from Tanger's boat."

Not two hundred yards distant, right below me on a shelf of white sand, amid sea plants and spindrift. It all looked substantial. There was no shimmer, no white glare. I hurried down the cliff.

"Paul!" the call came from the beach far behind, but I had no wish to respond. Perhaps the boat would tell—

Something bright white blew up in my face.

*   *   *

Three bearded figures in striped gowns squatted on a desert floor before a small tent. One in a red turban, one in a green turban, and one in a yellow turban. They rose in unison to stare at me, throwing their arms up as if to shield their sunburnt faces.

"A wizard. Plainly it is a wizard!" cried the one in the red turban.

"Perhaps a sorcerer," said the one in the green turban.

"Surely a necromancer," said the one in the yellow turban.

"I am none of those things," I protested. "I am just a man."

"Ah, just what a wizard would say."

"I am not a wizard."

"Surely the answer of a sorcerer."

"I am not a sorcerer."

"You speak the words of a necromancer."

They drew their scimitars.

"Slash the wizard's flesh."

"Stab the sorcerer."

"Smite the necromancer."

They surrounded me.

"Wait!" cried the one in the red turban. "The Head. We must ask the Head."

"Yes, the Head."

"The Head."

The man in the red turban disappeared into the tent to emerge with an ancient carved chest of dark wood.

"The Head will tell," he smiled.

"The Head knows all," the green one winked.

"It is a good Head," opined the yellow.

The one who held the box raised the lid. A bearded head was revealed.

"Now," said Red Turban, "are you in good voice, Head?"

He bent his ear to the lips of the head inside the box. There was whispering, but it seemed to come from the man holding the box.

"The Head says he is in excellent voice. I will ask him another. Head, will it rain today?" There was a pause while the man bent his ear to the lips. Once more, the whispering seemed to come from the man holding the box.

"The Head says it will not rain."

"He is a very wise head," Green Turban said, nodding at me.

"There is almost too much wisdom in such a head," said Yellow Turban.

"Now, Head," Red Turban said, "here is a wizard."

"A sorcerer."

"A necromancer."

"Here is one who arrives by magic in our land. How is such a thing possible?"

Once more he pretended to listen. "The Head wishes to know your place of origin," he said.

"I am from California."

"Head?"

He held his ear to the head in the box.

"The Head says there is no California."

"There is only here," said the second man.

"What is the name of this land?" I asked.

"Ah, it has no name."

"It has no name because of our enemies."

"No one can invade a land whose name he does not know."

"Therefore it has no name."

"The Head wants to know what took you from the land that does not exist."

"The flood," I heard myself saying, "the flood."

He bent his head to the lips. The whisper came.

"The Head declares that there is no flood within the memory of man."

There was a rasping sound, this time unmistakably from the Head. Now Red Turban did not bend his ear to the head in the box.

The Head spoke. "It is written that long ago a flood sent from the heavens washed evil from the land. Many died. How can you know of this?"

"All right for you, Head." Red Turban slammed the lid shut and flung the box to the sand.

On the ground, the head continued to mumble from inside the box.

"Sometimes it exaggerates," said Green Turban.

"It is not always to be believed," Yellow Turban said.

"It is a terrible Head," Red Turban averred.

"Sit," said Green Turban. "We will talk while we make you coffee."

"How is it that you speak my language?" I asked.

"Your language? It is our language."

"Where do you live?"

"The desert is our home," said Yellow Turban.

"Do many live here?"

"Only we," Green Turban said, "and our wives."

"We are simple shepherds," Yellow Turban said.

"Yes," agreed Green Turban. "We travel with our wives. Only today our wives are not with us."

"It must be lonely for you," I replied.

"You have not seen our wives," Red Turban said.

"Today we travel without sheep too." Green Turban poured coffee into three cups.

Yellow Turban explained, "We travel without our wives and without our sheep because today we are not husbands or shepherds."

"Today," said Red Turban, "we are murderers."

"Murderers?"

"Yes, but we must not reveal whom we will murder."

Red Turban said, "We would not murder anyone except he is a wizard, a sorcerer, and a necromancer, as well as a defiler of our land, who did not arrive in any flood, despite what the lying Head says." He kicked at the box, which made a hissing noise.

"I would not murder anyone," confided Yellow Turban, "providing he did one little favor for his three friends."

"Not only would I not kill one who did such a favor for his three friends," Green Turban added, "I would not even torture him."

"And I," said Red Turban, "for such a favor I would not make him eat the residue of what remains after the sheep have calved."

"A favor? What favor?"

"You must kill someone for us."

"He is our enemy."

"What has he done?"

"Oh, many things."

"He has stolen the moonrise."

"He has taken the wind out of the sky."

"He has melted the better stars."

"Here is our enemy," Red Turban said. With a quick movement of his finger he drew a picture in the sand.

"This is only a stick figure with a round head," I protested. "It doesn't look like anyone."

"I am not a professional artist," he sniffed, "merely a keeper of sheep." He disappeared into the tent and returned with what looked like a birdcage made of leather strips. It emitted a buzz like that of a rattlesnake.

"Look inside. Do you see this venomous insect?"

It was a scorpion the size of a lobster. It was buzzing, and bubbles came out of its mouth.

Red Turban said, "We will strap the leathern cage to the back of your neck, so you will be mindful of us while you murder our enemy. Do this quickly before the scorpion decides to put his sting into your neck. When you have killed our enemy, bring us his head, and we will remove the cage."

"Try not to annoy the scorpion."

Two drew their scimitars while the third fastened the cage.

"Why not kill him yourselves?" I asked.

"Ah, he may be our enemy, but he is also a friend."

"How will I recognize him?"

Green Turban spoke. "It did not appear so in the picture"—he turned apologetically to Red Turban—"although it is a very good likeness, but our enemy has the upper portions of a man and the lower portions of a horse."

"He's a centaur?"

"There are not many like him."

"Go across the desert between those little hills," Red Turban instructed. "Go quickly; already the scorpion sharpens his sting."

In a moment they were gone, along with their tent, and I wandered the desert alone to kill a centaur. Even as I trod the hard-packed, white, dazzling sand, the insect buzzed menacingly inside its cage.

A crowd of men in gowns and turbans lounged beside a pool at an oasis. They rose when I approached.

"I seek a centaur," I said boldly.

"Ah," said one, "we have no centaur here."

"We can offer a basilisk," his companion said. "Will not a basilisk do?"

"My wife's sister rents a hippogriff," said a third.

"Our village boasts a cockatrice," said another. "You will find it basking beneath the upas tree."

A burly white-bearded old man shouldered him aside.

"I know of a centaur," he said. "I will take you to it if you will bring me the fangs of the Great Serpent of the Desert."

"And I will show you the lair of that serpent," said one dressed only in a barrel. "But first you must bring me the Jackal with a Kiss like a Woman."

"I know many songs about centaurs," said a swarthy man with spectacles. "All of them exquisitely lyrical and improving to the listeners." He sang a few notes. "Wait!" he shouted. "What is that you wear upon your neck? You must love it greatly to keep it protected so." He adjusted his spectacles. "Ah, what a beautiful scorpion; for such a scorpion I would trade the Jackal with a Kiss like a Woman."

"And for such a jackal," declared the man wearing a barrel, "I would trade the fangs of the Great Serpent of the Desert."

"And for such fangs," shouted the white-bearded one, "I would take you to the Centaur!"

The one with the spectacles shouted at the one with the white beard, who shouted back, while the man in the barrel pounded its sides and shouted too. I found I was holding my ears against the din, when sudden cries split the shouting; dust rose from the desert, and the earth shook to galloping hooves.

"The Centaur! The Centaur!" everyone cried.

Something huge thundered on the horizon, the reverberation kicking up dust. A cloud of dust descended upon us, darkening the sun.

The crowd dispersed into the dust as Red Turban, Yellow Turban, and Green Turban appeared.

"The Centaur! The Centaur!" they yelled accusingly.

"I was about to get him for you," I shouted.

"Do not inconvenience yourself," said Red Turban, drawing his scimitar.

"We will do it ourselves," said Green Turban, drawing his scimitar.

"He is no longer our friend." Yellow Turban winked, drawing his scimitar.

"Hear him," one of them shouted through the dust. "He comes. He comes!" They raised their scimitars.

"He is here!"

Something like an express train thundered past in a whirl of dust, narrowly missing us, as the three pitifully waved their scimitars in little circles.

Then it was gone, and all that was left was the dust.

"It flees because I flashed the blade of my scimitar," said a voice from the dust.

"Mine clove the air with the voice of death," said the second.

"It cowers from the iron chill of my wounding steel," said the third.

The thunder started.

"Oh, ah, it returns, it returns!" they shouted.

Dropping their scimitars, they bolted into the desert.

"The insect," I cried. "It is still in the cage around my neck."

"Keep him," shouted a diminishing voice.

"We have no further use for him," said the second.

"He was not much of an insect," said the third.

The earth shook into a tremendous dust cloud. I was drowning in dust while I clasped my ears against the earthquake of hooves. Then it was upon me. As big as a building, its shadow towered over me, reared up on hind legs, the front hooves poised to strike.

I tried to see the beast before it trampled me to oblivion. To see a centaur, at least that was something, to see it before its hooves came down.

The dust fell. The air cleared. The centaur loomed out of the cloud, gigantic, rearing in the sunlight. It resolved itself into Donk Radlitt sitting on Henry. Then it collapsed to normal size.

The desert was gone. Donk was standing alone against the boat. There was silence in the little valley.

"I could see you the whole time, talking to yourself. You were in a light shimmery part, not a dark shimmery part. We'd better get back to the skiff now."

"It was like my medieval vision."

"Just be careful where you step. Those waves are all around us. What is that contraption strapped to your neck? It looks like a birdcage. Watch out for that shadow there. Jump for it!"

A black wave covered everything.

*   *   *

It was a mood rather than a place, a mood of dead, empty spaces, and dead, empty silence, because nothing existed to be seen or to be heard. It was a mood of nothing, endlessly afloat in a vacuum. The mood was all.

Sound spilled out, in a dry cachinnation. And there was sight. Dripping with red light, three cloaked, hooded figures bent over a bundle on the ground, beyond them a limited landscape of pointed rocks and darkness.

And there was feeling. Cold fingers fumbled with the leather straps around my neck.

The cage was taken off. Something thin and covered with black fur used gloved hands to spread a cape upon the rocky ground, deposited the cage on this, and disappeared into the darkness, while the three cloaked figures, no longer bending over the ground, grew visibly larger against the dark hills.

The insect crawled out of its cage, expanding till it grew as large as an ape, stood upright, and covered itself in the cape.

Once more the darkness closed in, as though an act was over.

I waited in a sightless, soundless darkness, in vacancy and nothingness, for the next act.

Lurid torch flames blew out of the dark, yet I could not discern the torchbearers, only the gloved hands that held the torches that lit the sharp rocks, the scorpion in its cape, and the cloaked figures, now far away but surpassing the hills in height.

The first figure inclined its head. Thin ropelike tentacles dangled from beneath its hood.

The second figure inclined its head. The hood fell off and revealed the head of a bear.

The third figure inclined its head.

But I turned away, for its yellow hair screamed of dark and murky waters.

I looked instead at the insect, now bent over the bundle that lay among the rocks. It was no longer a bundle but a prostrate human form. Crouching low, the insect sent a tube from its face into the body's open mouth.

The torchlight brightened.

And I saw.

With a wild scream I hurled myself against the monstrosity,

shoving it far into the void, while the next moment I lifted the body of Tanger Blake, everything screaming around me. High above, cloaked and hooded, the Three overlooked every action, as large as mountains now, white flames streaming from their heads, merging to the glowing outline of a thing with a high, peaked head. Then the picture flew into sparks as the torches expired, and I was in darkness, amid wild shrieks.

Abruptly there was light—Tanger by my side, back in the little valley. Beyond the trees the sea lapped gently at the shore. On the beach was Donk, shouting and waving to us both.

CHAPTER 24

Concerning Some Trees

t is always gratifying to be rescued," said Tanger when we were safe once more in the skiff and had pulled away from the island. "We tried to rescue you—Belle, Simon, and I— after we were driven from the land; the animals, you know. No sooner had you begun your exploratory trek than they emerged from the forest to gather into a perfect semicircle between us and the interior. At first they just stared. Then, very deliberately, they nudged us toward the sea. We got aboard the dinghy and left the shore. It was our plan to land secretly to pick you up once we were free of the animals. It never happened. A current seized us before we could get back to the shore, and swept us straight out to sea. We were on our backs while the dinghy plunged like a speedboat. On top of this, the world took on the appearance of a black-and-white negative; everything bright looked dark, while the dark things glowed. Strangest of all, the ocean changed from water into some kind of fabric. That's all the reality we had: the three of us in our boat inside a negative world, tearing through an ocean made of muslin that shrieked as it ripped apart.

"In no time the boat carried us here, never slackening its speed till it shot up onto the sand and we went sprawling into the middle of what looked like a crystalline cloud. Then began for me an endless phantasmagoria of lights and shadows. There was absolutely no succession of time. I know only that the lights and shadows eventually turned into a kind of place. There was someone there, a thin man in a cloak. You were there too, Paul. It is all quite confusing."

"What happened to Belle and Simon?"

"I never saw them again."

"We'll have to search the island," I said. "We found you. They must be here somewhere."

"For heaven's sake," warned Donk, "this time keep clear of anything that shimmers."

"Our rescuing them may depend on our entering the shimmering places," I said. "That's how I found Tanger."

"No," said Donk. "I saw him all the time that I saw you. Trouble is, I couldn't get to either one of you because you were both covered with shine. What saved you was that you rushed up against him and the two of you knocked yourselves onto solid land. Don't you be wandering into any more mirages. If your friends are here, we'll see them."

So we rowed back to shore, this time at another beach some distance from the first landing. The waves and shadows were a constant menace, yet we managed to avoid them. All we found were sand and trees, so we returned to the boat and rowed for another landing. The same happened, and the same. Two days passed like this.

"We can't find them," Donk said. "Let's go back for a search party. Maybe someone else will have better luck."

He was right, of course, yet it hurt.

"You can't exactly blame the animals," said Tanger as the three of us rowed for Grant. "They merely wanted us off their island. It wasn't the animals who shanghaied us to the shining place. It was more a malignant force. By the way, what happened to my cutter?"

"It disappeared," I said.

We put our backs to it, arriving the next day in the forenoon. The beach was deserted, so we made our way up to the settlement.

Belle, very pretty in shorts, lounged beside Simon on the village green. Nearby, two colossal men drank copious drafts of goat's milk.

Belle jumped up to hug us. "We've been here three days. We must have just missed each other!"

Butcher and Tea Presser, like two fabulous giants, had rescued Belle and Simon.

"There we stood on that same filthy island," Butcher said. "Right through that devil of a mirage we saw a bit of skirt flapping like a Union Jack."

"That was me," Belle said with a giggle.

"And all we had to do," Butcher continued, "was throw a bit of rope around some palm trees and tie the other ends around our waists—that way we could pull ourselves back. Ain't that right, mate?" Tea Presser nodded.

"Well, we had no sooner done so than we cast ourselves right into that shining demon—like diving into a pool, don't you know? Only here you couldn't see any bottom. Right, Tea Presser?" Tea Presser nodded.

"At first everything was as dark as the inside of a shark; it was like we had no eyes to see with. Then someone turned the lights on and planted a million trees. We were in the steamiest bit of swamp you could imagine—and insects swarming like they were being paid for it."

"When I first got into that awful swamp," Belle said, "I thought my worst trouble was that I was lost. I couldn't see much except the water at my feet because of the dim light and the hot mist that was everywhere. I had a feeling, though, that there were trees somewhere.

"I set out to look for Tanger and Simon. I splashed and waded, shouted and called, but all I got was deeper in the swamp. I knew something was terribly wrong. But what could I do? I had to find Tanger and Simon. I called and called, but the only sound I heard besides my voice was the splashing of my feet in the water.

"After a while I began to hear another splashing. At first I was overjoyed to think it was Tanger and Simon, and I called out to them. But they didn't answer, so I kept walking on, and all the time that splashing sound followed me like an echo. Suddenly it occurred to me that this might be the sound that something makes when it's stalking you through water. I went fast then, as fast as I could in that place, but the sound only got closer. I figured I'd hide behind a big swampy tree standing out of the mist a few feet away.

"When it grabbed hold of me, I knew I'd made the wrong decision."

"It was none of your namby-pamby domesticated oaks or ellums or larches," interrupted Butcher, "but a tree that looked like the devil himself. Crooked and spiky, with branches waving about like claws and with its cruel eyes wide open—a tree shouldn't have eyes—and its mouth opening and closing and full of spiky teeth made of wooden stakes, and all those branches—like a skellington's arms—drawing Belle closer."

"How did you get her out, Tea Presser?" I asked.

"Well," whispered Butcher, "all we had to do was to walk up to that tree and talk to it, man to tree, sort of. We asked it, squarelike, whether it wouldn't be a happier tree if it let the lady go. Isn't that right, Tea Presser?" Tea Presser guffawed.

"Don't believe them," Belle said. "These two nearly got themselves killed."

"Oh, well," said Butcher, "it was a troublesome tree. But in time Tea Presser and I convinced it of its erring ways."

Belle laughed. "Suddenly these two giants came along, attached to ropes that seemed to end in midair. They got me loose and pulled the ropes; only instead of the loose ends coming to us, we were pulled right into the real world once more."

"And not too soon either, eh, Tea Presser?" Butcher asked. Tea Presser smirked.

"Why was that?" someone asked.

"Why? I'll tell you why." Butcher's voice grew confidential. "I was too busy winding my rope to notice, but Tea Presser, he's a marvel for noticing detail."

"What did you notice, Tea Presser?" I asked.

"I'll tell you what he noticed," Butcher went on. "As we was winding away, Tea Presser looks up, and what does he see? He sees the whole swampful of trees suddenly come alive with eyes and mouths opening, and dragging their roots right out of the water, raising up their branches, and coming for us in a way that a whole army of woodcutters couldn't stop. That's what he saw. Isn't that right, Tea Presser?"

"But what of Simon all this time?" I asked. "Where were you?"

"I was the tree," said Simon.

"How's that?" said Donk.

"As soon as I hit that island, everything changed. I was in a swamp, and tall, and very hungry. There was meat ahead. From long experience I waded carefully, until I could get my branches around my lunch.

"It was clever, the meal that I stalked; it would move down the swamp a bit in a perfectly straight line; then it would give a sort of hitch and proceed catercorner, as though to throw me off the scent. But I was used to such maneuvers.

"The worst part was the competition. If the other trees scented the game, the competition would be fierce, especially from the older, more experienced trees, like Thad and Mule."

"Just like them," Burt put in.

"I don't suppose any of you has ever seen a tree fight?" Simon continued. "It's a horrid, splintering ordeal, and there is no quarter given till one of them lies roots-up, exposed to the merciless sun.

"I was not going to let this happen; I had gone too long with just a frog or two and an occasional fish caught by my lower branches. There was lunch ahead, and I wanted it all.

"Whenever another tree showed signs of interest, I pretended to be preening my roots; we all do this now and then; swirling through the warm water detaches stones and other debris that get lodged in the root system. So I fooled them as I stalked my game.

"Eventually I got her. She couldn't believe it was a tree that got her. That's always their weakness. I caught her in my branches and prepared to feast. That's when these two Australians showed up.

"No sooner do we start scrapping than the big one there"—referring to Tea Presser—"biffs me such a wallop, it lands me on my beam ends, exposing my roots to the merciless sun. 'Crikey,' says the other Australian, 'it's a bloke!' And I was. I was short, slim, my bark was gone, and I had a terrible pain in the jaw."

"Sorry, mate."

"By this time the other trees figured out they'd been tricked and attacked the lot of us."

"They were too many for us," said Butcher. "We roped and swung out of there. Then we rowed home."

CHAPTER 25

A Short Chapter

t is my suggestion," said Simon, "that for the time being we continue sharing our labor and talents, everybody helping everybody else, till we get far enough along that folks can work on their own. That sound all right?" (General acclamation).

It was the first town meeting since my friends and I had been reunited, a warm summer night after our community dinner. All twenty-five of us sat at long wooden tables inside the barnlike structure we had thrown up of stone and pine: Donk, Belle, Simon, and Tanger; Mac, Burt, and Burt's brother, Joe; Al the plumber, Butcher, Tea Presser, Sandra, Lou and his wife Mabel, Tom, Lolly, Minnie, Bedelia, Pete and his cousin Zachariah, Will, Opal, Pearl, Woodrow, Mr. Hanson, and I. Outside: Henry.

"We may not always agree on everything," Simon continued. Differences may arise; that's only human and natural. The important thing to remember is that we are civilized." Simon looked hard at all of us. "The one inexcusable crime would be for us to hurt one another. No matter what the argument between us, we must settle it with words, never with blows. Never, under any circumstances. Everyone agreed?"

(Thunderous applause.)

"What do we do if someone does?" Mr. Hanson asked.

"Toss him out!" cried Joe.

"Ship him over the horizon," said Butcher.

"Without a return ticket," said Belle.

(Unanimous applause.)

"The second point is this," Simon continued. "We've got to have knowledge, so we can grow our food more efficiently and build better shelters; so we can make a reaper or set a broken arm. And for a million other reasons. Knowledge is the blood of a civilized society. What I'm saying is, we need books. In someone's waterproof chest or abandoned cabin we may find a book that will make the difference between our failure and success. Right now we're parasites. Later on we'll have the leisure and the manpower actually to manufacture things—if we get knowledge, if we get books."

"Hear, hear!"

"While we're on the subject of knowledge," continued Simon, "I nominate Paul here to be our archivist and teacher."

(Applause.)

"We need books for another reason," he said. "For just plain intelligent reading to keep us from becoming brute beasts."

(More applause.)

"If we're still in a nominating mood," said Burt, "I nominate our eloquent speaker, Mr. Simon here, for the office of boss."

"Yes," said Butcher. "We do need a boss that will sift out the will of the people. I second the nomination."

"I really can't accept the responsibility," Simon said.

"That proves you're the man for the job," said Belle.

"Do we have an opposition candidate?"

Someone proposed Henry the horse, but Henry was discounted as being overqualified. There were no other takers, so Simon Girty became the first Boss of Grant.

"My first proclamation," said Simon, "is that we continue to send out exploring teams—both here and to the neighboring islands, to map the way and to look for books and people and—oh, for any good thing that is to be found. My second proclamation is that these teams be known as rangers. Thus I so proclaim; that is, if everyone's agreed."

"I recommend we steer clear of Flashpool," said Burt.

"Unless our boss gets lonely for his tree pals," put in Joe.

"Each one of us then," Simon went on, "will continue to work for the community, as well as prepare for some special, needed job that no one else can do. How does that sound?"

"I propose a more colorful wording," said Tanger. "Each of us shall ply his mystery: Paul, the mystery of teaching; Simon, the mystery of bossing; I, the mystery of engineering—or, in case of present need, of constructing. And so forth."

"As there's not much use these days for a plumber," Al said, standing up, "I'd like to announce my candidacy for the mystery of doctoring; that is, if I can figure out how to do it."

"The same goes for waitressing," said Belle. "I choose to be a ranger."

"And I a fisherman," said Tom, the former bartender.

"Put me down for selling used cars," said Burt. But he was hooted down.

"How come we don't have a preacher?" Mabel asked.

"That's right," said Pearl, "every community must have a preacher."

"Who's got a Bible?" Will asked. "Any Bibles left? Whoever's got a Bible is preacher."

Reluctantly Burt stood up. Shamefacedly. "I guess I have one in the cabin." So Burt was unanimously voted preacher.

The meeting over, we broke into knots of general conversation. Will got out his fiddle and played softly in the background.

Donk sat down on the bench next to me.

"I figured out the symbolism of your bear and squid," he said.

"How's that?" I asked.

"The symbolism behind their tug-of-war."

"What is it?" I asked.

"There is no reason for them to have had one."

Burt and Mac moved over to where we were sitting.

"Something's been bothering me about that Flashpool place," Mac said. "Are you sure the statue you saw was of one of those gugs?"

"Yes."

"Who put it there? And why?"

I shrugged. "As my old friend Hiram Bell put it, expect to see sights stranger than you've imagined. Maybe someday we'll know."

"By the way, Donkey," said Burt. "Since this is the time for general revelations—why did your parents name you Donk?"

"My name is Don Kenneth Radlitt. The *k* got too close to the Don and stuck there. Ah, there's Belle. Belle? What say to a walk?" She smiled beautifully.

"Let's all go," proposed Burt. "Who's for walking?"

We all went. Past the cabins and the meadows and the apple orchards, into the orange groves. The perfume of the fruit trees made one almost giddy in the warm summer night, as did the sounds of nocturnal birds and crickets under the benign moon. Someone took up a song. The night seemed to bless us.

CHAPTER 26

Saul

e were like children playing house. All the warm days we farmed our fields, planting from the remnants of Burt's garden or what we found on the land: turnips, tomatoes, lettuce, carrots, beans of astonishing varieties—while the orchards dripped with oranges, apples, grapefruit, and our gardens swelled with muskmelons, watermelons, cassava, honeydew, cantaloupe. While we farmed, others reared log cabins from the superfluity of timber, dug water channels, or fished.

Our first official coast rangers, Butcher and Tea Presser, brought back half a dozen feral sheep from the foothills of an island. The next team, Donk and Al the former plumber, returned laden with bushels of wild radishes. The third expedition fell to me and Belle.

It was three days' fair sailing in our little skiff toward the terra incognita of the east. The sea abounded in islets, mostly stretches of weedy turf barely rising from the waves. At midafternoon of the third day we drifted toward a towering ragged rock topped with a lushness of verdure visible from our skiff some miles away.

We landed smoothly in a little cove of soft sand and round white pebbles.

"Paulie," Belle said. "Let's separate to explore in different ways, and meet back here at sundown."

I didn't care much for the idea but agreed to let her have her way. So we divided up our supplies and marched off in different directions, she to explore the marge, I to investigate the interior of the island.

There was no real path, merely a way to slip between overly nourished tropical trees and their accompanying garlands of roots, creepers, and bushes I could not identify. After an hour or so, the jungle heated up.

I doubted that I would find anything here; possibly Belle would have better luck by the sea. Here was nothing but wet foliage. Somewhere ahead was the sound of running water. I made for this, because it was the only thing I could think of doing.

Abruptly the jungle ended in a welter of rocks at the edge of a gushing stream.

Sitting on a rock, fishing pole in hand, was the squint-eyed man of my vision. The same ugly frown. The same close-cropped black hair. He was barefoot, in overalls, and smiling the same mocking smile.

"The last time I saw you, you were swiveling a sword," he said sourly.

"And you were trailing a white beard!" I gasped.

"There I was, enjoying a peaceful kingdom," he accused in mock seriousness, "till you let the rats out of my knight. Why did you let the rats out of my knight?"

"Why did you try to feed me to your gug in the cellar?"

"Gug? I thought *I* made up the term. Well, I suppose it all has meaning, Mister...whatever your name is. Mine is Saul Dent."

"Paul Sant," I said.

"It would be," he said with a smile. "Well, Paul (if your name is more than a mere echo of my own), what brought you through the Wave of Waves?"

I told him some of my history.

"I was in a cave," he grimaced unpleasantly, "in perpetual darkness, with nothing but visions for company."

"You were in a cave?"

"Call it exploration. The rumble of the oncoming Wave must have caused a landslide to seal the entrance before the actual water hit. So all that happened was that I was buried low and dry a thousand fathoms from the sun. The darkness down there must have spawned the visions. Some were morbid." He shuddered.

"That's all over with."

"Some weren't so bad, especially that castle. I was as much monarch of those odd battlements as I would have been of real stone and sunlight. And all the time I was under the earth."

"How did you get out?" I asked.

He scratched his close-cropped head.

"You got me out," he said. "Every time I was snugly settled among my parapets and crenellations, you'd appear as an unsettling apparition, till at last I found myself flying backward through a tunnel straight to the surface. Whatever you did, I'm grateful, though at the time I thought you less a savior than a nuisance. By the way, what did you do?"

"I'm not sure," I said. "To me you were just part of the crazy fantasy, like the gug."

"I'm real." He smiled. "The gug was illusion."

"It was as real as you." And I told him of my war with the gugs on the whirlpool headland.

"And I thought my gug merely a delightful dream!" He shook his head in mock sadness.

His sardonic manner was so unexpected, I found myself laughing.

"It's a rum world we find ourselves in." He gestured at the rocks and foliage. "Rather tawdry. The effects are strained, the colors too intense. Take that sunset, for example; it is simply cheap. I could do it more subtly and at lower cost. The world has grown gaudy with bad art and lunatic visions."

"The supernatural is more prominent now," I said.

His eyebrows raised. "The supernatural? Oh, I see. You are joking. For a moment I thought . . . But you are too quick for me. Really, Paul. The supernatural?

"But yes," he added, "there are people naive enough to believe such things. There is in fact a certain amusement in the notion that our watery catastrophe was the result of an offended deity. Of course that would make Him a liar, because He promised Noah not to send another flood."

"What is your theory?" I asked.

"A geological upheaval. The world has had many, and of different types. Ice ages, asteroids slamming into the sea, earthquakes, volcanoes, electrical storms. We've had it all, and we'll have plenty more. It's the rent one pays for living on the planet. They are natural events, albeit a bit melodramatic. There is no mumbo jumbo involved."

His talk implied all the confidence inherent in the normal and predictable. For a moment I felt a dazzling relief in the thought of surrender to inevitable natural law.

"What happened this time," he continued, "happened before to cause the demise of the dinosaurs. Know what it was? The whole planet tilted, and the electromagnetic field that surrounds the planet and generates time got diverted. That's why time went crazy. For the same reason, evolution, which is a product of time, also went haywire and produced gugs and other oddities. This same electromagnetic field is responsible for all the crazy visions, because it got bunched up on top of itself and represented reality hierarchically instead of linearly. It is all as mechanical and as dull as a combustion engine," he said in his mocking voice.

"Must you debunk everything?" I laughed.

"You are right. Wait. I shall try to be humble. There. Now tell me where you live and what you do on this island."

I explained about rangering and told him of our accomplishments at U. S. Grant.

"A land of opportunities, eh? I may join you there," he said.

"Paul!" Belle's voice rang through the forest.

"A woman. Do I hear a woman?"

"It is Belle."

"A woman?"

"Belle Zabala. Belle! I'm over here."

"Where, Paul?"

"Keep walking, follow my voice."

Suddenly she was through the underbrush.

"Paul, I heard voices." She saw Saul. "I know you," she said.

"And I you." He smiled. "But from where?"

"I've only been in New York."

"Why, of course. It was New York. What part are you from?"

"Mostly the Bronx, but I've lived in Manhattan and various places upstate. I was a waitress at the Mile High Cafe."

"Why, that used to be my favorite restaurant. I went there with my mother. Remember me now?"

"We had a lot of customers."

"Sure. It was at the Mile High Cafe."

"Did you find anything, Belle, or have any adventures?" I asked.

"Nothing, Paul."

"Paul has found me, Belle. And I'm going to mean a lot to you both, a lot to everyone at—what is the name of your settlement?"

"Grant," said Belle uneasily.

"Grant," said the squint-eyed man.

CHAPTER 27

Old and New Ways

aul was immediately popular because of his outrageous irreverence and his gift for mimicry. He had a perverse and pugnacious willingness always to choose the wrong side of an argument. Yet, strangely enough, you often found yourself agreeing with him, not so much for his logic as because of his manner. He treated everything as a colossal joke, too big to be understood except by the very discriminating. Whenever you expressed an opinion contrary to his, up would go the eyebrows, on would come the look of quizzical surprise, saying that of course you were pretending naiveté—so that rather than be thought naive, you went along with what he said.

Right away he found fault with the solid and beautiful cabins we were crafting.

"Don't try to make things pretty or even long-lasting," he said. "The trick is to throw them up quickly so everyone has a house."

The eyebrows rose. "There is no functional purpose for decoration. What we want is shelter." Here he did a pantomime of a functional cabin that was so irresistibly funny, it doubled up the lot of us, and we followed his advice, although the patchwork shanties we threw up in half the time made us somehow ashamed. He led us with his self-deprecating, sophisticated air, and when that failed, he reached into his stock of glib, cynical jokes and inexhaustible impressions. We all laughed.

All except Belle.

"I know him, Paul," she confided to me, "in the way that someone knows—I don't know how to put it—an enemy. But I don't know how I know him or where I know him from."

"From the restaurant, he said."

"I'm sure it wasn't."

"If he was so bad," I said, "you would remember."

"That's the problem. I don't actually know him—but someone like him. Oh, I'm going crazy over this . . ."

But most delighted in his eccentricity. He was a combination of pundit and jester, always proposing extravagances.

"Look here," he said during one memorable meeting, "we need to protect everything we've built here. I move we form ourselves into an army."

"Good idea," someone said.

"An army? Don't you think we need all our time and strength just to build our community?" said Belle.

"Belle." The eyebrows rose. "We won't have a community if someone takes it away from us."

"Why don't we just farm and teach and try to be kind?" said Tanger.

"What happens when men with guns come?" came the mocking call.

"We don't know that there are any," answered Belle.

"But it won't hurt to be prepared, will it?" said Saul. "I mean, if we're armed, we don't have to use our guns."

"He's right," said someone. There were general murmurs of assent.

"We don't have guns," Tanger bellowed. "For all we know, there are no guns left on the planet."

"Ah, but we can make them," Saul said with a smile. "I know how to smelt iron and roll it into tubes. And we can dig saltpeter and sift it with charcoal into black powder. And we can dig flints." Some of the voices raised in admiration.

"Nonsense," said Tanger.

Saul's smile grew. "Right now," he said, "there are probably any number of groups of men searching the islands as we're doing; only they're not looking for books and plants; they're looking for conquest. We must have weapons to defend ourselves."

"Sounds reasonable to me. Just because we have guns doesn't mean we have to use them."

"That's right. It makes sense to be prepared."

"Look here," said Simon Girty, "we don't have time to go making guns that we probably won't use—especially when we've got planting, plowing, and building to attend to."

"How do you propose to protect our womenfolk when the attackers come?" The eyebrows rose.

"That's right."

Sandra, Mabel, and Lolly expressed the opinion that the womenfolk could protect themselves.

"Not against guns," someone argued. "No one can go up against a gun."

"We'll make guns," said Saul, "and, oh yes, in order to fight efficiently when the attackers come, we'll establish a military chain of command, separate from the civil." Here he launched into a pantomime, screamingly funny, of soldiers saluting one another and falling down.

"That's right."

"We hadn't thought of that."

"It's good to be prepared just in case."

"I wouldn't mind being a lieutenant."

"Confound you," said Tanger. "We have a leader—Simon. As boss he is the servant of the rest, not some strutting field marshal spitting out orders."

We put it to a vote, and Saul won.

Belle was not the only dissonant voice. Donk had just as little to do with Saul. "I do not care for Mr. Dent," he remarked one day as some of us were gathering stones for a wall. "I am a docile, peace-loving sort. Otherwise I would hang him."

"Everything that fella says makes sense," Mac joined in. "Yet it doesn't. He lacks common sense, Paul. And something else I can't figure out. Yet he has something."

"He is worldly wise," I said.

"We follow his ideas," said Tanger. "But are we any happier? I know, he makes us laugh, but the laughter evaporates, and there is only sadness. What do you think? Is Saul good for the community?"

"Good or bad," Mac replied, "I don't know what we can do about him. People don't have to agree with him. I mean, he's just one voice out of twenty-six of us."

Tanger hefted up his sack of stones. "Saul is influential because he embodies the comfortable delusion that one can laugh one's way out of anything. This attitude appeals to the old securities of invention, technology, and natural law."

"Like making guns and drilling an army," said Mac.

"I would still hang him," Donk said.

When later on I passed by Town Hall, I noticed Saul in a knot of men glancing furtively at a group of women and laughing about something.

Belle overtook me as I started toward my cabin.

"Paulie, we need to talk. Will you meet me at the orchard after dinner?"

"Why so secret, Belle?"

"The town is full of secrets, Paul. Haven't you noticed?"

There was a new moon darkening the orange groves when I picked my way that night among the trees beneath pale, metallic stars. The orchard smell was gone, and the air seemed somehow thin. Belle stepped out of the darkness.

"I'm off tomorrow, Paulie. I drew the lot of ranger. Tanger is going, too, but in the second team. I don't know how to say this, so I'll say it quick. That man . . . your friend Saul . . . I know who he is now."

"Yes?"

"He's the same creature who tried to make me kill my fish. The lemur. I'm sure of it. That squint in his eye is because of the apple I threw at him. The creature looks more like a man now."

"Who can believe that, Belle?"

"We can believe, Paul, you and I, because we know we live in a supernatural world. But Saul is doing everything he can to ridicule our belief in the supernatural. Sometimes I even find myself laughing with him. I get sick about it later."

"The one to go to is Simon," I said. "He's the boss."

"Simon isn't here now. He took a week off to go rangering with Donk and Henry. Joe's in temporary charge, and he wouldn't understand. I leave tomorrow. We need to discuss all this with Donk, Tanger, and Simon. We've got to bring it up at a town meeting."

"Sure, Belle. We'll discuss it when they get back. They'll know what to do. Meantime, I wouldn't say anything about it. What's the matter?"

"Paul, your eyebrows went up, just like his."

"I didn't mean it, Belle."

"Don't you believe me, Paulie?"

By the time I started my chores the next morning, she was gone. It was a dull day, neither hot nor cold, with a metallic overcast. Saul wheeled one of our makeshift carts.

"Hey, Paul. Lend a hand, will you? Simon said we're to play packhorse for a load of timber up yonder." He gestured toward the distance. "And, of course, whatever Simon says . . ." Here he did a takeoff of Simon. I didn't laugh.

Despite his increasing influence over us, for me Saul remained at bottom an absurd buffoon. Belle would meet only embarrassment and ridicule if she brought her preposterous accusation before the town meeting. Or worse. Her words might cause a division that would tear our community apart. I hoped her spell of rangering would put such matters from her mind. But I knew better.

We walked up the hill to what we called the broken forest, a lightning-blasted thicket whose splintered and uprooted trees were answerable to our crude tools. As we hammered our wedges through the cracking trunks, I pondered ways to protect Belle and our town and even the absurd man splitting wood with me. The answer came as I reached for a wedge to drive into a stump. What if someone else brought the subject up before Belle had a chance to? What if the whole notion evaporated while Belle was away? The words were out before I knew it.

"Saul," I said, inserting the wedge. "Suppose you suspected one of us was a creature posing as a man? What would you do about it?" I waited either for a facetious or a withering reply. He silently went on with his work.

"A sort of lemur," I persisted. "What if you thought one of us was a lemur masquerading as a man?" Again I waited for an answering joke.

He carefully put down the wedge he had been about to drive into a trunk.

"Has someone been abusing me?" A light gathered in his good eye and his smile was wide. "Is it Belle? Is it Belle Zabala, she of the brilliant intellect? Can't you picture her with Burt, arguing Kant's *Critique of Pure Reason* while exchanging fluids in the orchard? Look, like this! Watch, Paul, I'm Belle, and I'm rutting hard with Burt between my legs!"

I hit him. He went sprawling across the hard turf.

I helped him up. "I'm sorry, Saul. I'm terribly sorry. But what you said . . ."

He stood for a moment, tasting blood, before he kicked me in the groin. As I crouched shivering with pain, he threw up his hands and ran away.

I was left in the forest with my pain.

I resumed splitting timber, my mind confused and sad. Whatever possessed me to hit Saul? But how could he say such a filthy thing about Belle? My mind revolved as it had after I slaughtered the gugs. Why hadn't I blessed Saul, as I blessed the gug in the green chapel, instead of hitting him? But who thinks of blessing when the heart cries out for blood? Ah, but that's the challenge of it—when it is hardest—when you're mad to destroy. Maybe the next time, I said. Maybe the next time I will bless instead of strike. All it takes is a thought. The will. Remember. I felt much better now and went on loading timber. Perhaps Saul would return.

Someone crunched through the underbrush. It wasn't Saul. Butcher and Tea Presser emerged on either side of me.

"You have to come with us, mate," Butcher said.

"What is it, Butcher?" I asked. "Come to spell me for a while?"

"They want you," he said.

Silently they escorted me back down the hill.

Everyone was inside the Town Hall.

Joe and Mr. Hanson stood at the podium.

Tom brought in Saul. Even beneath the bandages I could tell his face and head were badly banged and swollen.

"Did you do this, Paul?" Joe asked, pulling aside the bandages. Saul's face looked terrible.

"No," I said. "Not that."

"Did you hit him, Paul?" Burt asked.

"Yes, but not like that."

"Why did you hit him, Paul?" said Joe.

"I'll tell you why!" Saul blurted beneath the bandages. "Paul thinks I'm a fish. That's it, isn't it, Paul?"

"No," I said lamely. "I hit him because he said something filthy about Belle."

"It was a joke, Paul—the same as when Belle told you I was a fish. It was only a joke, Paul."

"Where is Belle?" asked Mr. Hanson. "Let us ask Belle about this."

"Conveniently she is away on ranger duty," Saul said.

"Well, we can ask her about all this when she gets back, can't we?" Burt said. "After all . . ."

Saul stood up. "How many here think I'm a fish?" Here he pantomimed a fish, drawing cheers for being so game while battered. Suddenly he was serious. "Paul, I forgive you for what you did."

"It's what he said about Belle," I said. "And Burt, and—"

"They're my friends, Paul. If I said something bad about them, I'm sorry—even if both of them called me a fish."

Applause for being a good sport.

"I never said no such thing," Burt insisted.

"Saul, it may be like you to forgive," said Joe seriously. "But what he did is an outrage against the whole community. Remember what we agreed to at the town meeting when Simon became boss? A fella has no right ever to hit another fella."

"No matter what they done," echoed a chorus.

"It isn't a matter of apologizing," Joe continued. "This is the first mauling we've had. There can't be any more. You've got to go, Paul."

"Banishment?" I cried.

"Extra ranger duty," said Mac. "Just for a while. Would that answer, everybody?"

"Extra ranger duty," Joe agreed.

"Just for a while," Mac said.

"He kicked me and ran away," I protested.

"I'd run too if I got mauled that bad," Mr. Hanson said.

"I didn't do that." I pointed to the bandages.

Butcher and Tea Presser closed on me.

"The trouble with Saul is that he hypnotizes," I said. "Can't you see that? He's got you all on his side." Butcher put his hand on my shoulder.

"All right," I said. "I'll go. He's a hypnotist. You explain to Belle, Donk, Simon, and Tanger. They'll want to know."

"And we will tell them, Paul. Won't we?" Saul said.

Many of the townspeople said I should remain, but the matter was put to a vote.

"It's only for a little while, Paul," Mac said.

"Maybe a couple weeks," said Burt. "Like a vacation."

"We can't have people hitting other people," everyone said.

So I left Grant.

CHAPTER 28

A New Way

 chose a way untraveled yet by any of our party, toward the mountains whose white snowfields towered high and dazzling over the sunny orange groves, like a picture on an idealized citrus label. It was early morning of the next day as I threaded my way among date palms, then past the cornfields, my pride all the while smarting under the sting of banishment.

Yet I missed all my friends, even Saul. He'd bloodied himself up to prove a point, no doubt. I had a picture of him dashing himself against a rock, again and again, just to make a point.

So I walked on, that cool summer morning, and all that afternoon, taking a new way through a series of valleys, till I reached high ground and the pine trees came on thick and thicker; I tramped through a forest that never felt the sea. In the bright sunlight and fresh scent of pine the pang of banishment melted like frost, and I thought of my friends and the village of Grant; but mostly I considered the problem of Saul.

Hiram Bell might have been speaking of Saul in his lecture about people who put their trust in things that broke or wore out. The same smirking worldly wisdom, the cheap cynicism and easy ridicule. We are safe as long as we deride. Emptiness and lies. That was Saul.

Or worse, according to Belle.

I walked on long after the day ended, then sought shelter in my sleeping bag beneath a giant pine. I gazed up at the stars till sleep bore me away.

I started again at dawn, marveling once at a barrage of bluebirds firing at me out of the surrounding green branches. And there were deer. I wandered through forest and pasture and again through forest, with only my thoughts for company as I made for the mountains. Yet after many days the mountains seemed no nearer.

Then so much the larger and farther they must be, I said. I would eventually reach them. More days passed. For company I rehearsed the features of my life before the Great Wave, what had happened in such-and-such a year, month, day, till the events of my life glowed like a gallery of newly cleaned portraits. At length I came to pine-covered foothills and, planting my feet in the soft earth, began to break a path up a carpet of slippery pine needles. And all the while, as I trod higher up the steep slope, my mind read the book of my life before the Wave.

I panted in the thin air, my hands reaching out to gain a purchase on the boulders that now dotted the slopes. Brown lizards scampered on the rocks or rustled among the needles at my feet while I scrambled up the foothills toward the looming peaks ahead. Once I looked back to the shine of the sea; but all the land was green and indistinct. About me I felt the warm mountain.

Now at last I was deep in the mountains, trudging through vast meadows, then up again to find footholds in rock. Sometimes I came upon what seemed an ancient path, but it invariably dwindled to a mere animal track.

Sometimes I slept. When I awoke, I took food from my pack. In one fair spot, water ran down in streams, splashing over rocks, spilling into deep, trout-filled pools. Bushy-tailed squirrels made almost mechanical noises from the branches. Always I made for the highest ground through a succession of days and nights, higher, the portraits in my head glowing with color. The air turned colder.

My mind became a library of all the beings I had seen in flesh and in vision. The head crabs and gugs were real, I said. The silver fish was real. The bear and squid were real. What about the three men and their scorpion on Flashpool Island, were they real? As real as Simon's becoming a predatory tree. As real as Belle expelling the lemur. And what of the thing in the Volkswagen? Was it real too? I paused, shivering with cold, to dig the sweater out of my pack. The ground was cold with snow.

I tracked over snowfields, crunched up vast slopes, pushed through drifts of powder, pulling myself ever higher by what holds the rock suggested. I was weary beyond description, yet I kept on. At sunset I puffed up a steep incline to find myself on a plain, perfectly flat, beneath a blood-red sky, while a blood-red sun stained the snow the same color. There was nothing above but the fire of the sky. I had reached the top.

Bone weary, near fainting with fatigue, I trudged through the snow toward the steep cliff side and gazed down into a red world of mist and shadow. The slanting sun threw my shadow into the mist, which somehow multiplied it into countless images of me as long as the mountains were high. In the thin air the penumbra took on a reality. Once more I saw the events of my life, but less as portraits now than as archetypes pointing to the significance of things.

I found myself lying in the snow, confronting my life beyond the Wave. There was Bell and the Great Fish, and there was the thing inside the yellow Volkswagen. I was being told the why of it. There was a promise too. This is tremendous, I told myself. You must remember, you must remember. If only I could form the thoughts into words and carve them into stone. The silver fish told me something. This time, it said. Remember the design of things. Bell and Belle. Nothing happens by accident, except free choice. Remember. But I was fast asleep and could not remember. Just before I woke, the snow turned soft and dry, like the cotton snow that covers the base of a decorated Christmas tree. I could see electric Christmas lights clipped to branches. And from other branches, hanging on wire hooks, were enameled figures of my friends. But there was one whose hook had slipped, and he now lay cracked and broken on the hardwood floor.

I do not know how long I stayed on that snow plain; but I think there were not many more dreams. All I know is that I ate and warmed myself, and eventually I shed a cloak I did not know I had, before I began the long steep way down the other side of the mountain to the mist-covered valley.

The way was free of snow, and I made good progress for the better part of a day, the valley growing warmer as it came up to meet me. The mist thinned as I descended, till suddenly it was gone, and I could see the valley below.

Three buildings mounted on an island of pavement dominated the valley floor, the whole surrounded by forest and hedged in by snowcapped mountains. Three buildings deposited like flotsam at high tide, transported here by who knows what bizarre subversion of physical law—loomed incongruously amid the pine trees and brushwood. I ran shouting down the remnant of mountain that separated us. I was met with no answering cries and expected none. Such was my experience after the Wave that I no longer expected anything.

I was down and onto the pavement, looking up at the three buildings in an even row. They were new, clean, undisturbed by wave or weather. Wild with exhilaration, I dashed into the first.

It was a grocery store. The perishables had long ago yielded to nature. But I met an infinity of canned goods, neatly stacked on the shelves, not one can on the floor. I seized a can of peaches, then had to find the kitchen aisle for a can opener. I drank the syrup first, then let each peach drop into my mouth. "I'll be back," I said to the beans and the soups. "Look for me when I get here," I laughed, waving to the stacked jars of peanut butter.

I ran out and into the next building, the department store, and dashed up the escalator, taking inventory of the different levels. I felt like Crusoe—better yet, like Adam in Paradise. Clothes. Tools. Camping gear—enough supplies to keep us going until we learned to make them for ourselves.

But the last building was best. I believe I howled as my feet bounded up the stairs and through the many halls. The mellow smell sent my pulse racing. Floor after floor, I dashed ever higher through the lofty, precious corridors. For the last building was a library.

The Orgy

It was a prayer unbreathed, answered beyond expectation.

All the knowledge, the beauty, and the wisdom of the human race lent their perfume to the air. Here I found medical texts for Al; for Tanger, the technical sheets and specifications for melting copper, pouring concrete. Did Belle want a garden? a vineyard? a plantation? It was all on the shelves—the accumulated wisdom based on the results of a million experiments —the fruits of thousands of years—all for the taking. Would we breed goats? Irrigate a wheat field? Smelt iron for the coulter of a plow? The hard labor had been done. The notion was planted, watered, nurtured a hundred times over with lifetimes of labor. The fruit was all ours.

I reeled intoxicated through the corridors. Banked like a choir, in ascending tiers stood the music books. Scores of the *Ninth*

Symphony. The *B Minor Mass. Così fan tutte.* Magic tomes to transform the brain to instruments, soloists, conductor, as the eyes scanned the page. Oh, and there, in a big mahogany cabinet I discovered a collection of real musical instruments! No more would we have to make do with Will's homemade fiddle. I caressed the fine scrollwork of a highly polished violin lying in its bed of crushed velvet. The next shelf held a viola. The big closets on the sides housed a cello and bass. And there were piccolos and flutes, clarinets and bassoons, and brass too, trumpets, trombones, and horns. I closed the cabinets lovingly and went on through the corridors.

And found the glories of English literature.

I could not have known the hunger had I not beheld the feast. It was a saturnalia. It was an orgy.

In a time of dread, scarcely secure within wooden walls, men clustered around their chief, defying the darkness, drinking mead, singing heroic tales of a dark time older still; while without brooded the eternal forest. Three times something crept in while the heroes slept, to eat the flesh from their bodies, until Beowulf, discharging uncanny power, tore off the monster's arm. In murderous revenge crept the creature's appalling mother, stalking through the boggy mist to steal into the hall to slaughter the sleeping heroes. Cased in steel against the monsters of the deep, Beowulf swam the flood, pursued the horror to its underwater lair, and slew it with a hero's sword.

I plunged into the rainbow of Chaucer, into the Middle English that was always more beautiful than any modern rendition, toward the place where people *goon on Pilgrimages.* My companions all about me, the Wyf and Miller on one hand, the Knight on the other; the Franklin, Sumnour, Chaucer himself, all of us alight in the warm medieval rainbow, from the Wyf's scarlet stockings to the Prioress's *peire of bedes, gauded al with grene;* and *broche of gold ful shene,* and the *Yeman's sheef of pecok-arwes brighte and kene*—the whole gaudy, noisy, life-proclaiming procession tempered by the sanity of mine host, Harry Baily.

Now into the chessboard cosmos of Malory, the telescopic flatland of Logres, folded to foreshortened perspectives of forest and fountain, castle and court; inhabited by the magnificent, the mighty, the noble, the malignant, the crafty, and the base, everyone fired by lust or aspiration, fueled by chivalry or treachery; all accompanied by the clash of armour as jousting knights to-brast their lances to crash to earth in deadly combat with swords. It is Galahad, the Knight of the Grail, whose passion burns most ardently, for it aspires to grace, whereas his father, Lancelot, is incited by earthly love; Galahad finds the Grail, Lancelot has only Guinevere. Central to all is the tragedy and ambiguity of Arthur, victim of a doom beyond his making.

Then to the Mighty One, deeper than them all. Read his contemporaries—Marlowe, Jonson, Fletcher, and Greene—to know how far he surpassed them. Webster imitated him, Tourneur, but not to his height, no, nor ever to his depth. The phrases stand straight up out of the page, transforming sullen Earth into something rich and strange—slubber the gloss, the sledded Polacks, all candied o'er. It is poetry that surprises. Unfolding in a universe as high and deep and wide as literature can go, the plays perfectly satisfy because they contain all.

Then on to Milton, who aimed higher than his predecessors in aspiring to things unattempted yet in prose or rhyme. The blind bard elevating the highest story in the highest style, triumphantly depicting literary impossibilities, like Satan swimming through chaos to work his spite on God's best work. Or the opening scene of the fallen angels, abashed in a metallic hell, while Satan looks on with baleful eyes. And Adam having everything, the conversation of angels, friendship with God Himself, the companionship of Eve, most beautiful, most glorious, most desirable woman, with the admonition to propagate lest he risk divine displeasure! Yet Adam lost all but Eve and for no reason on his part, unless Eden were too good to keep. Sometimes it is less painful to stop reading just before Adam's Fall, in the ninth book.

Then a visit with Johnson, wisest and best man in the world. The man to take your troubles to. Are you plagued by fear, uncertainty, the threat of death? Consult Johnson. Sir, he will impart the treasures of his mind as well as the felicities of his tongue. "It matters not how a man dies," quoth Johnson, "but how he lives. The act of dying is not of importance, it lasts so short a time. A man knows it must be so, and submits. It will do him no good to whine." And thank God, you will say. Doctor Johnson felt this way too about pain and poverty, uncertainty and fear. Only poor Johnson; as an impoverished, half-blind, and friendless young man, he had few to allay his fear. He had only his great mind and masculine courage. Despite poverty, infirmity, and the bewildering torture of compulsive behavior, his courage, deep learning, and solid common sense prevailed against chaos and inspissated oppugnancy. And the rougher side of Johnson, sparing neither tusks nor claws when mauling his opponent in verbal argument, and growling where he cannot maul? This is Johnson when he is least secure and, in a sense, most vulnerable; it is the attribute that separates the real Johnson from the romanized statue of St. Paul's Cathedral. The wisest man I know.

Open the pages of Keats. Keats, with his puns and pantomimed musical instruments, the maker of wonderful things where wonderful things did not exist. Where were the magic casements? The peak in Darien? The lady with the wild eyes?—before Keats called them forth to exist? He said he was half in love with death. But he was totally in love with Life and Poesy and Fanny Brawne. He said he was half in love with death because at the time death was far from him, but when his lungs spewed arterial blood, he wasn't even one-quarter in love with death. But he accepted it at last, before he was twenty-six, just as he had accepted the challenge of poetry. He was the most a poet can be.

Then into another universe. The cosmos of Dickens. Larger than mere worlds, Dickens populated galaxies. Quilp, Pickwick, Micawber, Squeers—a mere planet cannot hold them, any more than a closet can contain Apollo. The alchemical transcendence of squalor into splendor. The poetry of dirt and fog and buttered toast and milk punch. The mythology built of unwashed humanity and insane humor.

Into the ecstasy of Arthur Machen. A mysticism like Thomas Traherne. The sense of wonder and strangeness. The sense of the unknown. The desire for the unknown. Living life like a sacrament; joying in Caerphilly cheese, the good cider of Gwent, the hiero-glyphic of literature, the poetry of London, the strangeness of ordinary life. He takes you to Caerleon, where the Usk winds in mystic esses, and you can look up at the holy mountain of Twyn Barlwm. He leads you through subterranean lanes to the sculptured earth of the Roman amphitheater. Look up, you can see the wild mountains of the White People, the Great God Pan, the Hill of Dreams. He makes you wise, sane, and good by imparting the rich-ness of his sanely mystical and elevated mind.

I fell back exhausted. More of a swoon, in which all came to life, tumbling onto one another, into an order chaotic—yet that made sense as part of the divine purpose of the universe. All night Beowulf fought Gawain, Mr. Pickwick courted the Wyf of Bath, while Keats conversed with Shakespeare, and Johnson roared with mirth. I woke early without hangover to drink from other bottles.

The days passed in the mansions of literature. I would rise at dawn, float upon a Wyatt sonnet, then go bathe by a clear stream that washed a corner of the pavement and wound far into the sea of forest. Then on to grocery shopping and breakfast usually by the stream, now and then carrying my lunch high into a mountain, to share the time with friends—Coleridge, Hazlitt, Lamb, De Quincey; other times Addison, Pope. Usually Johnson, often through Boswell's brilliant stagecraft. Sometimes the great modern fantasists: Lovecraft, Machen, Blackwood, Dunsany, M. R. James. Or G. K. Chesterton or C. S. Lewis on God or literature or life, then a rearward plunge into the classics—the *Odyssey, Iliad,* or the hubris and hamartia of Aeschylus and Company. Weeks must have passed. I did not mark their passage.

The world was sane and real. It was Eden before Eve. If I lacked the fellowship of angels, I had my books to content me. Someday, I might find my Eve. In the meantime here was Paradise. Here was perfect happiness.

I lived the seventeenth century: Bacon and Burton and Browne and Fuller's *Worthies of England* and Donne—most passionate of men—in love with girls and God, passionate about both. Herrick, whose poems were passionate about girls but whose life was passionate about God. Lovelace, who produced only three masterpieces, and Walton, whose life was a masterpiece. Only gradually did I think of Grant. Only gradually did the faces of my friends rise before the printed page. Donk Radlitt should know these books firsthand, a thousand times more potent than any renditions I could supply. And Belle, Tanger, and Simon, and Burt and the rest. What was it Simon had said? We need good reading just to keep us from being brute beasts.

It wasn't as if they needed me. I didn't suppose I was missed much, except by my closest friends. Yet I owed the community the treasure of the library as well as my other finds. They would have real clothing now instead of the homespun stuff they'd had to make do with. They would have the medical books and all the good things inside cans. By now Burt was probably a preacher and could make use of the huge theology section. The tools would be a god-send.

From the department store I loaded a knapsack with hammers, nails, screws and screwdrivers, cold chisels and vise grips. For myself, I selected the biggest bowie knife I'd ever seen, with a gleaming blade made of surgical steel, almost a short sword, fitted into a leather scabbard fastened to my belt. If I must go back, I would do it with style. Reluctantly, I started out, the more anxious to deliver my goods and return to my books.

CHAPTER 30

The Golden Calf

hy are they all so quiet? I asked the night air as I made my way through the orchard. This was Saturday night. Where was Will's fiddle? The clapping hands and laughter? The night was empty. The fields were empty. Except for the fences. Everywhere I ran into fences posted with signs, but the thin moon provided too little light to read them by. The land had a barrack-and-barbed-wire feeling.

Against my hip the bowie knife in its leather sheath felt reassuring. Where was everybody?

I looked in at the Town Hall; it was dark and deserted. I felt strangely reluctant to go around to the cabins and knock on doors, lest all should prove empty.

The best thing to do, I supposed, was to go to my own cabin and wait for morning. I skirted the darkened cabins of my friends and stole over to the far side of the clearing, where beneath the shadows of the surrounding pines my cabin stood perfectly dark, perfectly still.

I knew it was occupied even before I banged the door closed behind me.

"Who's there?" I called, reaching through the darkness for the lamp on the shelf, and fell sprawling over something—a chair—that was in the wrong place. Something like a bear trap clashed over me as I fell to the floor.

I tried to raise myself by the chair, but the chair was torn away with a force that sent me sprawling halfway under the bed. I lay stunned, while above me something chopped at the mattress with giant hedge clippers. I gathered my strength to heave the bed up, throwing it onto some thrashing muscular thing, pinning it down for an instant, and reached for the bowie knife.

I could not keep it long pinned down. The hedge clippers kept working, tearing the straw from the bucking, heaving bed, while I bore down with my body to keep the bed between us and drove the bowie knife through the straw mattress and right into whatever was making it move. I stabbed like a harpooner, hitting with everything I had till the chopping stopped, and the bed stopped heaving. Even then I did not stop, but stabbed until my arm fell limp.

I reached over to a hanging lamp and struck flint to steel. In the glow of light I pulled what remained of the bed off the thing I'd killed.

It was a gug, and it was clothed in a sash. The hedge clippers had been its jaws.

I began to shout then. I shouted till voices rang outside, and the door burst open. It was Lolly.

"Lolly," I cried. "Thank God. Look!" I was shaking. "I killed it!" I sought her warm sympathy.

Instead, she put her head back out the door and shouted, "It's Paul Sant, and he's killed a humanal!"

Mr. Hanson stuck his head in. "Murder," he said.

"He murdered a humanal," said a voice outside. "Pete, Will, Woodrow. Paul Sant snuck back here and killed a humanal."

Saul came in. He was wearing some kind of gray uniform. "You won't stay away." He shook his head sadly. "You have to injure someone. Now you have murdered."

More voices from outside. "It's Paul Sant, and he murdered a humanal." The voices seemed dreamlike, as through a haze of hypnosis.

Butcher came last. "Some people don't learn," he said roughly. "We've places for your type, mate."

"The police are here," said Lolly.

Four gugs came through the door, sashes slung around their middle parts, grotesque hoods surmounting their peaked heads. They began to hiss.

"Jail," Saul barked. "To jail."

They took my knife from me. I was marched outside to the far end of our wheat field and thrust into a solid stone hut.

They had actually built a jail! Something firm wedged the door shut.

"It's our first murder, Paul," came Saul's voice out of the dark. "We're off to discuss it."

Something moved in one corner of the dark cell. This time I had no weapon.

"Is that you, Paul?" Mac's voice.

"Mac?"

"His very self. I see they got you too. What'd you do? I got drunk on some peach brandy I made."

"Mac, this is insane. A jail? Police? And gugs!"

"It don't seem intelligent at that," said Mac's voice. "Yet there's got to be laws, otherwise there's no civilization."

"This madness is hardly civilized," I said. "Where's Simon? Why doesn't he put a stop to this?"

"Simon? What for you want to tell Simon? Simon can't do no good. Saul is boss now."

"What happened?"

"Saul convinced them that having a one-party candidate isn't exactly a free election. He said you've got to have at least two candidates. Simon said he didn't mind if what we did expressed the will of the people, so we had a special election with a secret ballot. Saul won."

"Who counted the votes?"

"Why, seems to me I can't rightly recollect. But they was counted all right."

"Where was everyone when I came back?"

"Well, except for me, Outpost 1 (they don't call it Grant anymore). Outpost 1 was empty because practically everyone was out spying on the foreign army that landed a few miles away. Saul says they're here to take over, and we ought to get them before they get us. We can do it, too. We've guns and ammunition now, that Saul showed us how to make. And we're all soldiers, trained to fight; that is, if the gugs (I mean the humanals) don't get them first. Saul said gugs is an insensitive word, and that we should call them humanals, to let them know they're as good as us. Anyhow, he was all for sending the humanals to attack the foreign army, but Tanger, Simon, Belle, and some others said we ought to make sure first the army's hostile. Saul says we can send in the humanals fast and take prisoners, and then if we see they're friendly, we can let them go afterwards with no harm done. But we did a hand vote, and Saul lost out. He got so mad, I thought he'd turn those humanals on us, but he only smiled and said we'd lose the element of surprise, and they would get us sure."

"I still don't understand what happened," I said.

"It's all different now," Mac said. "Saul is different. Remember how he was always making jokes? Everyone's serious all the time now. He has some kind of power. Over those humanals and over most of us. Why, he has Butcher and Tea Presser under his spell, and Lolly and Mr. Hanson think he's some kind of Moses. And I'll tell you one other thing: There's fear running around like a epidemic."

"Donk wouldn't put up with this," I said. "He'd hang Saul first. Where is Donk?"

"As soon as Saul started talking about free elections, Donk lit out with Henry. And when Saul was elected, Burt and Joe left too. Likewise Al the plumber. Belle, Tanger, Simon, and I stayed behind, figuring someone with common sense ought to."

"Was it Saul who brought the gugs?"

"Yes, one Saturday night, right before the party was supposed to start. 'Look, everybody,' he says, 'I've got something here that no civilized society should be without.' And he starts laughing.

"Some of the womenfolk was like to faint when those things stalked in wearing pieces of cloth around their scaly bodies. But Saul lectured them.

"Sure, they look different, he says; their values may be different too; but other people's values are just as true as ours. We got to get along with all life forms. These humanals want to work alongside us as members of our community. All they need is to get back into the water every hour or so, to stock up on oxygen. I tell you I never saw Saul so eloquent; it was a regular sermon. He mentioned you. Paul Sant, he says, called these people gugs and told you they were vicious and cruel. Well, wouldn't you be vicious and cruel if someone called you gugs? It's how we treat people that determines how they act. You call our friends here humanals—their true name—and we'll all get along fine. The worst thing you can do is hurt another's feelings.

"Heck, most of us knew they was only glorified sharks. But the way Saul said it made us feel so mean, we was ashamed not to have those things around, even though they scared some of us half to death. The funny thing is, they did bring in fish; they brought in more fish than we could use. We had so many, we got to using the fish for fertilizer. You should have seen the way those gugs herded those fish. They'd get way out to sea and form a kind of wall and just swim in. And the fish? They just beached themselves on shore, almost as if they'd prefer suicide to the company of a gug, I mean a humanal. Why, the gugs was so handy, Saul even had them doing manual labor. Who do you think built this jail?"

"So you worked side by side with the gugs," I said.

"Not hardly. Saul laughed one day when he saw a bunch of us working with them in the field. Why should we work? he says. Let them do the labor. And he winks and points at the gugs. Let them sweat under the sun while we do important things like civic planning.

"It didn't seem right, us not working, and we couldn't do much in the way of civic planning either. Saul did all that. And somehow he made it seem only natural to turn those gugs into police and soldiers too. The worrisome part is, he's the only one that can communicate with them. Why're you here, Paul?"

Something hissed outside. The door swung open. It was Will. Behind him four gugs stood in readiness.

"They're all waiting at the meeting hall," Will said nervously. "You'd better come, Paul. Mac, you get to come too."

The Town Hall was nearly full. Belle was there, looking white. Mac, Butcher, Tea Presser, Sandra, Lou and Mabel, Tom, Lolly, Minnie, Bedelia, Pete and Zachariah, Will, Opal, Pearl, Woodrow, and Mr. Hanson sat on benches facing us.

"After all," someone was saying, "he might be judged innocent."

The dead gug lay stretched out on a board. Beside it four other gugs kept guard. Saul stood at the dais. Behind the dais someone had erected a screen.

"The law is everything," said Saul. "Nothing's bigger than the law. If we don't satisfy the law's demands, we are savages. The law is everything.

"I know as boss I should remain impartial to judge the case; yet since I'm the only one here with legal knowledge, I ask temporarily to be relieved of my office as boss in order to express the case for the State. After which Paul can tell his side; then we can decide his innocence or guilt."

"What's the punishment if he's found guilty?" Mac asked.

The faces looked away.

"Banishment didn't work," Saul reminded. "He returned."

"Maybe he'll be innocent," whispered the jurors.

"Then it's agreed." Saul smiled.

"What about self-defense?" Belle's voice.

"Let the trial proceed," said Saul.

"Who are the humanals?" He gestured toward the four gugs standing beside the dead one on the board. "The humanals are our helpers. They depend on us to civilize them while they make their upward climb to evolution. In exchange they work for us, build for us, gather fish from the depths of the seas for us. As well, they risk their lives to protect us. They are our police, our army, our companions. All they ask in exchange is tolerance. Tolerance!"

"Did you kill this humanal, Paul?" asked Mr. Hanson.

"You are out of order, Mr. Hanson," Saul cautioned.

"Did you kill the humanal?" Mr. Hanson repeated.

"It tried to kill me."

"Did you kill him, Paul?"

"Yes. It was waiting in my cabin."

Saul spoke. "What business had he in your cabin, Paul?"

"None. It tried to kill me," I heard myself say again.

He appealed to the assembly. "How many of you have ever seen a humanal try to kill—or even threaten anyone?"

A general murmur. "None." "Never." "Only fish."

"You lured him into your cabin, didn't you, Paul? How did you do it? Did you tell him you needed help to lift something? Humanals are always willing to help. Is that what happened?"

"He—it tried to kill me," I lamely repeated.

"Why did you murder him, Paul? That remains the question. Did you murder him because he looks different from you? Because he speaks a different language from you? Did you murder him because it offends you that a person you think a member of an inferior species should mingle as an equal among our community? Is that it, Paul? Was he to have been an example to all such inferiors who do not know their place?"

"Don't listen to him!" Belle screamed. "He mixes everything up. It's all lies. He's a lie. I've told you over and over. He's not even a man. He's a thing!"

The eyebrows went up pityingly.

"Belle, in this case, I more than anyone would like to ignore the law. But once you ignore the law, there is no law. You excuse a murder here, next a rape, an incest; then pillage and mass execution. Where do you stop? Obeying the law draws the line between civilization and anarchy."

He faced the audience.

"You see the victim at the murderer's feet. You've heard the murderer himself confess. Did he or did he not commit this crime?"

"I reckon he done it, all right." General assent.

"Paul, I sentence you to death."

Screams.

Saul was raving. "You can see that, Paul, can't you? You have to die, for the good of the community. For civilization. Think of Socrates and his hemlock. You broke the law. No one is above the law. Take the body away." The four gugs carried the body behind the screen.

"Now, what form of execution do you prefer?"

"How about being talked to death?" It was Donk standing at the back of the hall.

"If Paul's a murderer, we are slaughterers," shouted Tanger, stepping into the hall.

"We just blew apart a whole army of gugs." It was Simon.

"Gug soup," said Donk.

"They tried to massacre us," said Simon.

"Right after we decided not to massacre the foreign army we had been spying on."

"When the gugs saw we weren't going to shoot down that foreign army," Simon said, "they charged us—us and the foreign army."

"You're not being clear," said Tanger. "The gugs died nobly to protect us from the desperate and depraved foe. Behold the enemy."

Eight children tramped in.

"These are the sinister field marshals," continued Tanger. "Notice their cunning. Masquerading like children. The noble gugs tried to protect us from them. Being ungrateful, we shot those gugs to pieces with the firearms Saul made for us."

"The gugs was going to kill the little children?" asked Lolly, wide-eyed. "They're monsters!"

"Watch what you say," said Mac. "To hurt someone's feelings is the worst possible crime. Remember, all values are equally true."

The rest of the foreign army tramped in. Young men and women, middle-aged and old, undernourished but laughing.

"The gugs would have eaten us all if they could," Burt said. "Maybe now they're not so hungry."

Donk stepped over to the dais. "Let's have another look at exhibit A," he said, whipping away the screen.

The four gug guards were busily devouring their dead companion.

"These walking horrors of hell!" exclaimed Mr. Hanson.

"I made a mistake," Saul said with a laugh. "I was wrong and I acknowledge it. Here. Here is Saul making a wrongful, stupid mistake." Here he tried mimicking himself as the trial judge. No one laughed, so he stopped. "After all," he said, "I only thought of the good of Outpost 1."

"You mean Grant," Butcher said.

"Grant." "Grant?" came the murmuring from the assembly. "What happened to Grant?"

"You were willing to murder Paul," Joe shouted, "for killing one of those walking sharks?"

"It was my zeal for tolerance," Saul protested, "the very pith of civilization. Have I not restored cherished institutions?"

"All I know is that we were happy before you came," said Mabel. "We're miserable now."

"We're afraid all the time," said Lou.

Butcher stepped up to the dais. "Nothing's funny anymore, Saul." He turned to me. "Paul, I'm sorry."

Tea Presser was weeping.

"We lost our common sense," said Mr. Hanson.

Will grabbed my arm. "Paul, that fella, he got us all confused— we thought we was doing right."

"Goodbye, Saul," said Belle.

"Don't be in a hurry to come back," said Lolly.

"Don't merely leave Grant. Get off the continent."

"Get off the planet."

Saul's face was a mask of hate now. His hands curled to claws as he tried to reach Belle. I stepped between them.

Saul grabbed my arm, and whispered in my ear. "You think you've won, Paul. You haven't won. There's one who waits for you . . . in a yellow dress inside a Volkswagen. She's waiting, Paul."

He dashed out. We all followed. The sun was rising as Saul ran past the orchards, across the tilled fields, and toward the ocean. The sun's red face lit him as he scampered like an animal, we vainly trying to keep up. Light was everywhere, rays shooting up and around the sea cliffs. Saul, nearly on all fours, darted toward the precipice, with the sun gleaming on each boulder, penetrating even the caves near the summit. In the increasing red glare, Saul dived between the bottommost rocks and disappeared into a hole in the ground.

CHAPTER 31

A Theory and
a Sermon

he gugs left when Saul did. We tore
down and burned everything associated
with him. Then we extended our re-
sources to accommodate our growing population. There were sixty-
two of us now, including eight children. Saul had called the wave
of immigrants an army; so it was, an army of educated, kindly
people, eager for citizenship in Grant. Before we built half their
cabins, we had to adjust for another invasion—a party of twelve
men and women, and four cats—arriving on a flotilla of makeshift
canoes. Their first action was an offer to share their few potatoes.

As chief chef, Donk was consulted.

"How shall we prepare them?" asked Lolly, his second in command. "Mashed, baked, fried, french-fried, or cottage-fried?"

Donk squinted and scratched his head.

"Let the ground eat them," Donk said oracularly.

"Meaning?"

"Plant them."

So we had potatoes from then on.

One day a new settler arrived with a boatload of hens and roosters fluttering about his improvised henhouse. We dubbed him the chicken man. At the same time Butcher and Tea Presser returned from an expedition, dragging what Tanger characterized as "an exaltation" of hogs.

When Henry disappeared, Donk was inconsolable. He slunk about the community, trying to maintain an air of imperturbability, though certain parties claimed to notice a decline in the quality of his cuisine. As days passed, Donk got lower and lower, pretending it was the weather depressing his spirits.

After two weeks his patience broke.

"Hang it," he said to nobody in particular. "I'm going after him." But before Donk left camp, Henry returned, three comely mares trotting by his side.

It is amazing how much work we did. Getting the crop in was the most important project, that and building shelters to house our increased population—honest-to-goodness little cottages now, made with brick and straw thatch. We worked all day and even by torchlight. Belle saw to that. It was also Belle who found an easier route to the library, bypassing the mountains, so you could walk there in a few days or get there sooner if you rode Henry or one of the mares. We brought a great many books back to the branch library we established at Ulysses S. Grant, the demands of work not permitting most of us the leisure for many journeys. Will, Joe, and Mabel studied horticulture, multiplying our orchards and reinvigorating our fruit trees. Most learned farming. We had enough food to export now, if there was anyplace to export it to.

Similarly, all helped themselves to the treasures from the grocery and department stores, against the time when we should have leisure and expertise to manufacture such things.

I, whose work involved scholarship and research, spent most of my time at the library, returning only to discharge my teaching obligations. Al the plumber often accompanied me to the library in order to ransack the medical section, doing his best to learn how to drill teeth and set bones. Sometimes Tanger went along, to consult sources on technology and engineering. So while Tanger explored food production and power plants and Al dissected imaginary specimens, I labored to record the history of the world since the Wave.

Tanger appeared one morning after breakfast when I was preparing to return to the library.

"I'm coming with you to test out a theory," he said. But he would not discuss it during our long trek to the library, informing me instead of his progress in converting the iron so recently used to make guns into machined parts for an engine to generate electricity.

"Of course, all is contingent on our raw materials and what we can make of them. The wheel must precede the bicycle; the rubber tree and rubber technology must anticipate the tire. Then, have you considered the labor and complexity involved in manufacturing a spoke? Do you know what I would really like to have? The one book our library doesn't stock. Don't laugh. It's your old friend Stoddard *On the Steam Engine*. I read it in college. It speaks in terms of the primitive technology we have today. If I had a copy, I think I could build a steam engine." He laughed. "Possibly a locomotive." Our journey continued, he putting me off with lectures in technology every time I returned to the theory he was anxious to test.

Eventually, when we reached the valley and stopped by the grocery store, his behavior grew strange. He walked through the store declaiming loudly, almost boasting of the secret he was about to impart. He did the same in the department store. Furthermore, he insisted we walk around the buildings, all the time alluding to his great discovery.

I thought he made an unnecessary amount of noise in the library. Never had I seen him so clumsy as he walked through every floor. Once he let a great tome fall from the shelf, so the impact boomed and echoed up and down the corridors.

It was not until we were snugly settled in the main reading room, the largest and with the most doors, that Tanger broached his subject.

"I have been thinking some more about time." His voice was very loud. "Particularly about the accelerated time that remade the world around us, but that bypassed us as the Angel of Death did the children of Israel. Our friends the gugs are a product of accelerated time; the same goes for your head crabs and other oddities. Yet there is no visible alteration of Henry and the mares, or of the other livestock we've encountered, which makes me think they probably came through the Wave as we did, and like us remained constant in time. In other words, time stood still for the people and higher animals that survived the Wave, while the rest of Creation— including sea fauna—went hurtling forward at an incalculable rate. Such a conclusion I could at least provisionally accept." His voice sank so low that I had to lean forward to hear him.

"What I cannot accept," the quiet voice said, "is the inconsistency of the time process on inanimate things, namely, the buildings. Some structures we found intact, whereas others were nearly sawdust. The place you stayed at in Head Crab Land was intact. Mr. Bell's cabin was intact. It is the same with Burt's cabin, which floated him here. On the other hand, there is Belle, who encountered only the ruins of the farmhouse, and Mr. Hanson, plowing through debris drifts in sawdust city, or Will and his mountain paradise of termited lumber. You can see the inconsistency. Why should some buildings crumble with age while others retain their vigor?"

His voice was normal now except for a certain edge of excitement.

"My theory is this: in every case of a surviving building, an occupant was either in the building when the Wave hit or must have reached the building before time shredded it to splinters. In other words, human contact kept the buildings in the same time frame with us. Don't ask me why this is so."

"But I occupied only one cabin on Head Crab Island. Why didn't the others fall to pieces?"

"Apparently your spirit or personality infected the area—in a nice way, of course—and kept the neighborhood in the same time frame as you. Is any of this credible?"

"It is if it happened."

"I had got so far in my speculation when a sort of ontological house fell on me. Granting my hypothesis was true, that what preserved a building was the presence of a human being inside it, the question arose: What preserved the building you and I are sitting in?

"This is a library, Paul," he said in a deliberate stage whisper. "I am thinking there must be a *librarian*"—he emphasized the word—"one who by now must realize we are kindly, civilized men"—he raised his voice again—"incapable of a harsh word, let alone incivility."

There was a sort of giggle behind us. Like a doe from the forest, gaining confidence as she meets no discernible threat, a slim, dark girl, wide-eyed behind her spectacles, slipped from between the stacks.

"My name is Mary," she said meekly. "I am the librarian here. I've practically lived here since I was a girl." She blushed. "I still live here." She paused, as if embarrassed about something.

"My name is Tanger Blake," Tanger said, smiling. "This is my friend Paul Sant."

"I've seen Mr. Sant." She blushed again. "And you, Mr. Blake, and many others here. I hid myself. I wasn't sure quite what you wanted." Again a doe.

"Right now we want you to verify a theory of mine," Tanger said gently. "Were you occupying this building when the Wave hit? If not, can you tell us how soon after you made it your home?"

"It was a wave, then?" She settled in an armchair next to me, sitting on her heels.

"I was at my desk upstairs. The day had been very warm, so I had the windows open, even though the traffic was noisy below. Since I had work to do, I didn't much notice the peculiarities of weather, till I became aware that I was hearing a very different sound from the noise of the traffic. It was like a lot of people snapping their fingers. I put my work down and went to the window. A cloud cover had settled in, and little threads of light were sparking all over the sky, as if it were raining electricity. A crowd had gathered outside to observe the phenomenon, but I had my work to finish, so I was content to watch from the window. After a while I returned to work.

"I took a break after about an hour. By then the cloud cover had separated into individual shapes that looked like the designs on a paisley shawl. They were moving rapidly, back and forth like fish in an aquarium. Again I watched, fascinated, then realized I still hadn't finished my work.

"When I looked up again, I nearly screamed. The cloud shapes had become faces—almost cartoon faces, not human, not animal. They hung in the sky, thousands of them, then they began to slide down, like gelatin transparencies, right onto the buildings, the cars, the sidewalk. The air grew coated with them, obscuring the city.

"All except the department store across the street and the grocery next door. They were clear. My building too. I put my head out the window and looked up. I saw something like hands over the three buildings—you know the ones by Albrecht Dürer? Then, as I watched, the other buildings on the block began to crumble. Their walls gave way; the ceilings collapsed. The whole city fell. I have the impression too of rains and snows, and of the world growing dark and light, dark and light.

"The city was gone. A snow-covered mountain dominated the whole world. For the longest time that's all there was—the three buildings, the snow-covered mountain, and I. Then the mountain started to move. The glacier ran down the sides," she laughed, "like melting ice cream while the mountain bumped along, till the mountain scraped itself down to nothing and became part of the plain. All that was left of civilization was some pavement, a few traffic signs, and the three buildings in the middle of a landscape that could have been on the moon.

"The rock began to break. Except for one inclined plane, the whole moon landscape divided into fragments, crumbling to smaller and smaller bits, finally into powder. A flood of water came pouring down the incline, immersing everything in sight. The water left, and the world was green. I looked away a moment from the window. When I turned back, a forest had grown up.

"I realized I was perfectly happy. Deer were actually running down Main Street. I didn't move; the world had moved around me. I set up housekeeping in the department store, though mainly I lived in the library. I saw you all. I hid. I guess I was afraid." She smiled mischievously as she held up a book. "Right now I'm reading Donne."

Mary, her few things packed in a valise, returned with us to Grant. She took over my teaching tasks so I could get on with my chronicle. Her presence seemed to cast a spell. I remember she sat between Tanger and me that rich evening, the night Burt preached his first sermon.

"I'm reading from Genesis today." He cleared his throat.

" 'And God saw that the wickedness of man was great in the earth, and that every imagination of the thoughts of his heart was only evil continually.

" 'And it repented the Lord that he had made man on the earth, and it grieved him at his heart.'

" 'And the waters prevailed upon the earth a hundred and fifty days.' " He laid the book down.

"That's what the Lord done," Burt said, "because of our wicked ways. But after everything got good and dry again, the Lord felt sorry." Here he took up the book again.

" 'I will establish my covenant with you,' the Lord told Noah; 'neither shall all flesh be cut off any more by the waters of a flood; neither shall there any more be a flood to destroy the earth.'

"In other words," said Burt, "whatever happened to us, the Lord had no direct hand in it, so we must have done it to ourselves.

"Now here's my thoughts, brethren and . . . er, sisters. There were always folk stealing from other folk, and scaring them, and hitting them, and breaking into their houses, and damaging their property, and hurting them in all kinds of ways, as well as being just plain rude. And there was other folk just as bad with their busy-bodying and self-righteousing—always telling other people what to think, what to do, even what words to say—that the whole planet just got top-heavy with sin and collapsed under the avenging waters."

(Cries of "Amen.")

Burt smiled with encouragement.

"And I also think that irregardless of all the bad things we done, the Lord done His best to help us. That's why he led us here to the . . . ah, Promised Land." (More cries of "Amen.")

"And he give us to eat of the fruits of the earth, with our trees that were already growing when we got here, and the wheat that we'd have throwed away if it hadn't been for Donk." (Cries of

"Hooray for Donk!") "And the beans and things that growed in Joe's and my garden and just floated along here with our other stuff.

"And all the good things our new friends brought, the taters, and the chickens that the chicken man brought, and those hogs that our Australian friends found, not to mention the whole darn grocery and department store and library that Paul found, which from what I hear we owe to the little lady here." (Mary blushed.)

"What I'm saying, dear brethren and, er, sisters, is that the Lord's been bountiful to us, in spite of our sometimes being ungrateful for His bounty, and I think we should be more beholden to the Lord by working hard and respecting other people's lives and property, and most of all, by not bossing people around."

"That all you got to say?" asked Lolly, standing up.

"That's all," Burt said.

"Why, then, amen. You're the prettiest preacher I ever heard," she said with a smile.

"Amen," we all said. And there was general backslapping and congratulation, until someone remembered that the service was still in progress, so Burt led us in a hymn, which Will accompanied on his fiddle and Simon on the flute that he had taken from the musical instrument collection in the library.

It was the richest evening I had spent since the flood, but not because of Burt or his sermon. It was the richest evening, because I held Mary's hand.

CHAPTER 32

Old Friends

It was the eve of our harvest celebration, and a few of us lounged about the Town Hall admiring our decorations. The crop was in, everything snug within its barn or bin, the fields gleaned, the animals bedded down, all like Keats's bees, who "think warm days will never cease, / For Summer has o'er-brimm'd their clammy cells." Will, who led the dance committee, assisted by Mary and Tea Presser, had just pronounced the decorations complete. Gorgeous with pumpkins, squashes, and cornshucks, the hall was a temple to autumn. Reluctant to leave, we stood admiring the study in red and russet, eager for the next day's celebration, which would conclude with the harvest dance.

Pete and his cousin, Zachariah, came flying in, followed by Belle and Butcher.

"We saw somebody," Pete said excitedly.

"Come poling out of Black Swamp," his cousin added. "We went back to Black Swamp to have a look, and there they were, standing up in a skiff, poling in the dark waters under those dark trees, all in shadow."

"We think it was Saul," said Pete.

"And he wasn't alone," said Zachariah.

"We couldn't see them clearly, because they were far away, and mostly in shadow, but the one with him might be a lady wearing a bonnet."

"We called out and lifted our hats, but they didn't even look up."

"The skiff just passed by."

"Where are they now?" asked Belle.

"We don't know."

"Find them," she said.

"We don't know for sure it was Saul."

"Find them."

"And don't be too gentle about it," said Butcher.

They quickly formed what Donk called a welcoming committee—Belle and Tea Presser, Mr. Hanson and Will. Donk carried a rope. Pete and Zachariah led the way. "I told you nothing good would come of Black Swamp." Zachariah's voice faded into the distance.

The welcoming committee found no trace of Saul or skiff or female companion. It was a mirage, we said, a will-o'-the-wisp compounded of swamp water, creeping shadows, and miasmatic mist. So Saul, skiff, and companion faded like ghosts into conjecture. We put such thoughts to the back of our minds and talked at dinner of nothing but the harvest celebration. After dinner I returned to the hall to survey some last-minute decorations. Mac stopped by.

"I saw Saul," he said, "and that other that's with him. They were just outside, right by the big barbecue. I saw Saul, and spoke to him. But I knew before I said a word, it wasn't anything but a shadow, a tired, thin shadow that disappeared when I spoke to it."

"I saw Saul's ghost," said Simon, entering, "along with someone—something—he had by him. A shape, muffled. Its head swollen. Could be a bonnet. It looked larger than Saul."

"The one I saw was smaller," said Mac.

"Could be it's growing," Simon said.

We got up a little search party in the dark. But we found neither
Saul nor ghost, only a few errant moonbeams straying in the
October night.

By four the next day, I had spoken with three more persons who
claimed to have seen Saul. Al had seen him the evening before,
pacing the stubble of a gleaned field by twilight, a smaller, bent
figure in tow. Joe saw him that morning in the orchard gliding by
the trees. Lou saw him at noon in the wood field where I had
knocked him down. In every case the vision vanished when it was
addressed.

Many of us went about our work that day dreaming of the splendid celebration to come, the October sun barely creeping across the
fields as we chopped or hauled wood, fished the streams, and built
shelters. Others, though, thought of Saul and wondered.

It was glorious that night. The outdoor feast had been sumptuous, with every manner of side dish our ingenious cooks could fur-
nish. The wine pressed from Mac's vineyard flowed. We had had
some music already, a Haydn string quartet, played by some of our
latest residents on the instruments found in the library. There would
be banjo and fiddle music later at the dance.

Euphoric, the whole community sat outside at the picnic tables.
Overhead a full harvest moon lit up the grounds like a floodlight.

Mary was next to me. Belle sat on my other side. Across were
Burt and Lolly. We were in the midst of general conversation when
Belle's hand gripped my shoulder.

Saul and a muffled figure stood not three feet away. The whole village rose to its feet.

Donk was the first to speak.

"One word from you, Mr. Saul, one word ever so slightly oblique..." Here, seemingly from nowhere, Donk produced a rope.

"Goes for me too, Saul," said Simon. Butcher and Tea Presser left their places.

Saul looked insubstantial in the burning moonlight. His companion stood near him, in a gray dress, her face unrecognizable beneath a deep, closely fitting bonnet.

"You'd better leave, Saul," Tanger said sternly.

Saul's voice seemed to come from a great distance. "My mother," he said, nodding at his companion. "She's sick."

"Get them out of here," said Belle, appalled. "Get them both out of here!"

"Maybe you'd better have a look, Al," suggested Simon.

"No," said Belle. "It's a trick."

Al escorted the muffled figure inside the Town Hall, while we argued our course of action. The two of them returned moments later, Al looking dazed.

"She's awfully old," he whispered. "And she's sick, all right. Very sick." I thought he would faint, but he recovered himself and stood shaking in the moonlight.

"Reckon we can't turn her away," someone said.

Belle turned to Saul.

"You clear off anyhow, Saul."

Saul seemed less like a ghost now.

"I've learned my lesson, Belle. I won't try to be boss anymore."

"Get out, Saul!"

"I went to see Mother right after I left you, Belle."

"Put him in a boat," Belle said. "Put them both in a boat." The muffled figure turned toward Belle.

"Poor Mother," Saul said, louder. "There was little to eat, and she had grown so thin. We lived in a cave, you know. 'Mother,' I said, 'We have to find you another home.' She didn't want to leave."

"Beware of your pity!" Belle shouted at us.

"It was terribly stupid of me to try to be boss. I was wrong about the humanals, too, I mean the gugs. Do you know, they've all returned to the sea?"

"Get out, Saul," Belle hissed. "Take your mother with you."

"I got her to leave the cave, though, and we wandered, she and I, all over. But there was never enough to eat. I said there was lots of food here. Now we're back."

"What's the matter," asked Belle, "can't she talk?"

"Oh, yes. She can talk, all right, can't you, Mother?"

The eyes seemed to glow beneath the bonnet.

"She can talk when she wants to," said Saul.

"Land sakes," said Mabel. "We ought to feed them. We ought to feed them both."

"She's just a sick old lady," said Lolly.

"Maybe we can keep her for a while, but he has to go," said Mr. Hanson.

"You can't separate a boy from his mother," said several newcomers, who had not known Saul.

"Saul, if we relax our laws a bit and permit you to stay until your mother can travel, will you promise to keep the peace?" Simon asked.

"Oh, yes, Simon. Yes indeed!"

"Get them out of here!" Belle shouted. "Sink them both beneath the waves."

"We all know what he did, Belle," Mabel said. "But she's a old lady."

"She didn't do anything to us," Lolly said.

Simon spoke. "What do you think, Zachariah?"

"I think nothing good can come from Black Swamp."

"Maybe he's got gugs around," Joe said. "You got gugs, Saul?"

"No sir, no gugs."

"And no guns?" asked Mac.

"No guns."

We discussed it. Belle, Donk, Butcher, and some others were for instant banishment. We put it to a vote, and the mercy party won.

Belle retired in defeat.

CHAPTER 33

Perilous Times and Peaceful

We rarely saw Saul after that, he and his mother retiring to a lean-to they had thrown up somewhere in the vicinity of Black Swamp. Several of our women offered to nurse Saul's mother, but only Al was permitted to do so. Al grew close-mouthed and sullen as he made daily visits to the swamp; whenever we inquired about the old lady's health, he answered in a monotone that she was improving but not yet fully recovered. Many of our women pressed lunch baskets upon him to deliver to the invalid, but he always returned them untasted, saying she had found something she liked better. And all the while Al grew worse, losing weight till his skin was tight on his skull.

One night he wandered into the village, in a dead fear, sick with fever and raving that we must send a party to the swamp to set fire to the hovel.

"Burn her," he whispered. "Burn them with cleansing fire."

We put him to bed and nursed him. He was quiet by morning, but his memory was gone of Saul and his mother and of the time spent in Black Swamp.

Mr. Hanson and some others made a trip to the hovel the next day, to see if we couldn't send someone to take over Al's job, but Saul met them at the door to say his mother was nearly recovered and that they would soon be leaving.

Life went on. Al recovered and was back at the library studying medicine. But he never regained his memories of Saul's mother (who he claimed did not exist) or of what went on in the hovel at Black Swamp. For the rest of us, we heard no more from Saul or from his mother. Someone went to inquire at the hovel but found it empty and ruined. We concluded that Saul and his mother had silently stolen away. After a while they were nearly forgotten.

I had a dream. I saw Saul's mother, her bonneted figure by moonlight in a cemetery. She stood against a tomb whose stone glowed white while in her gloved hands she held a folded document that made sense of everything. It was her intention to read from this document as soon as the right moment arrived. I had been waiting patiently for the reading, throughout the long night, from the earliest blackening of the sky to the moment when the moonlight bleached the tombstones to a blinding white. After a while, to pass the time, I took to studying the names on those tombstones, titanic names, I could tell, but carven in a language unknown to me. When I at last looked back to Saul's mother, she had the document unfolded. Beneath the bonnet her lips began to move.

"Mother wants to talk to you," a voice said in my ear.

Saul stood by my bed. It was morning.

"We are leaving," he said. "She has a message for you."

Saul had invaded my cabin.

"She doesn't know me," I said, groggy.

"I know you. Mother has something important to tell you."

"I can't go," I said. His eye took on the brightness of the tomb-stones in my dream. "It's impossible," I said. I found myself dressing hastily. A moment later, I had followed him out the door.

It was not so much the dream or the glow in his eye that had me trudging after him across the fields and beyond into the woods. It was more the sense of something unfinished. Not a word was passed as we plodded miles through bush and timber, wading streams, working through foliage that shut us off from the world. The light died altogether as we twisted our way down through tree-hung passages into a wasteland of mud and creepers. Water was everywhere. It was as if all sunshine and stability had been siphoned from the earth, making the world a dismal, cold, never-ending slough of dripping vegetation. At some time we boarded a skiff, and Saul poled us farther into the black, wet waste.

"We had to abandon our little home," Saul said. "Mother found the visitors disturbing."

"The visitors?"

"Not your sort, Paul." We moved farther into the festering heart of all that decay. Saul left the skiff tangled in creepers, and we felt our way inside a rain cloud of foliage, to stand up in some sort of shelter, whether natural or artificial, I could not determine. Its dark and cavernous rooms seemed endless. Yet some were lit after a fashion; the sodden walls and ceilings diffused the glow of rotting things, while all the time there was the sound of water gurgling just out of sight.

I sensed rather than saw her. The dress covering the entire body. The bonnet concealing the head. She seemed larger now. Saul's voice came over the gurgling water, almost monotonous in the cold half-light.

"Mother wants to take you with us," said Saul.

"Where are you going, Saul?" My voice sounded lost in the rotting darkness.

"You call it Flashpool. We have another name. It is your place of burial. Mother's going.

"I was buried once, Paul," came Saul's voice. "You rescued me. It was I who came out of the door you obligingly opened."

"The door?"

"The iron vaults that once were ships, once beneath the waves. My voice led you. I was sealed by—I can't say the name. I used to know the air. Thank you. There are beings like you and beings like Mother and me."

"I know your purpose!" I shouted. "It's to spoil everything we do. All you have is spite."

The voice was pitying. "All we have?"

"In the days before the Wave. You and your kind, with your sociology and other pseudosciences, getting us to believe we were insignificant parasites, empty of substance and spirit."

"It usually worked. In your time, we usually won. We lost because of the Wave. Now we'll go back to the old way. The old way is better. Goodbye, Paul." Saul's voice came from far away. "Mother will talk to you now." Saul's mother stepped out of the darkness.

The shelter was gone. The swamp was gone. Overhead, a black sun threw thin shadows on a lifeless expanse giving way to a flat and empty ocean.

Saul's mother stood with her back to me, facing the ocean. As she raised her hand, the water tore apart like tissue paper. The bonneted head gave me a backward look, then she went gliding into the sea, skimming over the dry felt sea bottom, I running behind her, fingering the stuff that a moment before had been waves.

Beneath a black sun, I hurtled through a negative landscape of dry fabrics, my head bursting with visions of that open trapdoor beneath the metal caverns. All I knew was that I had opened the door and must close it. I must seize the one fleeing before me and bury it beneath the earth, and set a stone above it. Once it was gone, I could deal with Saul.

Sometimes I gained on her, and the muffled figure loomed larger on the brown flat, till I could almost have embraced her. Then she would shoot far ahead, to the very edge of the horizon. The brown felt sea bottom shot by in level monotony, while the black sun gave no more heat than sunlight. The world was cheap fabric, stretched taut and splitting till the whole horizon suddenly tore across like rotten cheesecloth, revealing a rise of fabric cliffs, topped by a fabric statue brooding over the fabric sea. I had reached Flashpool Island.

Saul's mother was gone. I peered everywhere around me. The brown sea bottom was gone. The fabric had changed to rock and earth. All that existed was the cliff before me, topped by the stupendous statue of the gug, larger now than could have been possible in the actual world.

Then I saw her. At the base of the statue was an entrance. She stood a moment there, then disappeared inside. I gained the cliff, hurling myself after her. It was dark. It smelled like a cave. Stone steps led down into the earth, down perhaps to a trapdoor.

I followed down, ever down into the dark, till the steps gave way to bare earth, and still the path led down, shrinking to a narrow hole, and farther down and down still, till I was so far underground I knew I could never climb up. The cave smell was gone. The smell I now smelled was of all the graveyards of the earth, and I knew at last that I had reached the end of things. There was nowhere left to go but into the cul-de-sac at the end of the tunnel, the last little bit of space. So I ducked my head and felt metal, and climbed into a cramped space.

I heard the once familiar sound of a car door slamming. The lights came on. I was in the passenger seat of a Volkswagen. Saul's mother was in the driver's seat. As she turned her head toward me, the bonnet slipped off.

A wealth of golden hair fell over the putrifying face. I choked on the smell of decay. Her eyes turned into lighted flames.

There was a grinding of earth, and the tunnel collapsed around us. We were buried together beneath the earth.

I screamed from every pore; my stomach screamed, and my head screamed, and my mouth and heart screamed. The rotting thing caught me in its embrace and kissed my mouth.

I was swallowed, inside its stomach, crammed with the bones and hearts and fragments of broken humanity swirling about me as I spiraled backward down its digestive tract.

Suddenly I thought of Mary and Hiram Bell, and, oddly enough, of that tremendous silver fish, thundering from the waters, to erupt into the dazzling sunlight. And I blessed them all. And, for no reason, I blessed the thing that had swallowed me, and I blessed Saul, the gugs, and the world of slimy darkness.

An explosion tore the world apart and left me staggering outside in sunlight. Gone were the black sun, the negative transparencies, the false fabric look. The gug statue was blasted to shards. Flashpool Island was substantial.

Saul lay trembling on the beach, looking rather like the lemur he had been when Belle found him in her garden. Yet unmistakable was the close-cropped head, the squinting eye—squinting, one would think, almost in triumph.

"Sant!" he wailed. "I hid a gun under a floorboard at Town Hall. It has three bullets. One for Belle, one for Mary, and one for Henry, because I hate horses. Sooner or later the survivors will send a boat for you, but those three will be rotten by then. Goodbye, Paul."

Before I could stop him, he was into the surf and nearly halfway to the horizon. I could only look on.

Suddenly I heard him scream. The silver fish had surfaced and hovered on the water contemplating Saul, motionless now in the waves. Saul screamed again as the fish gave a sort of chuckle, audible from the shore, and made a great leap, swallowing Saul and diving deep under the sea.

The waves subsided, and the sea was calm once more.

I was marooned here, till somebody should send a boat, but such things no longer mattered. Mary was safe, and Belle, and dear Henry. We were all safe from menacing powers. The sunlight felt good; the rock did not waver. What happened to me no longer mattered.

I gave a passing look out to sea. Someone was headed right for me. I climbed a rock to have a better view. In the distance was a flat craft, manned by a small black figure. For a moment I thought it was the silent rower of my vision, where I first met Saul.

As the craft drew nearer, I almost fell off my perch. It was my old platform. And the figure was Hiram Bell. I waved and shouted.

He rode the platform right onto the beach, all the time roaring with pugnacity and joy.

"Paul! Paul! This is Valhalla! You live, every inch a hero. Is this your Ithaca? Where is Penelope?" He thundered off the platform and onto the beach, where we embraced and shook hands.

"I've much to tell, Paul. I had skirmishes with monsters—half sharks, half lizards."

"Gugs," I said.

"Ho, a perfect name. Bring on more gugs, I say! Paul, it was joy!"

"How do you happen to be here?" I asked, laughing. "Where did you get my platform?"

"Now, Paul, you speak of that platform with reverence. To answer your question, I did not get your platform; your platform got me; it came all the way back to pick me up, because it has a mind of its own. You know, I never really looked at it when you first rode it over to my isle. I figured it for the top of some pier or pavilion. But when it returned, I took the time to examine it. The wood and the workmanship and the antiquity struck me immediately as similar to something I saw once, something that does not often permit itself to be seen. The platform is only a small part of it, of course. The rest of it is probably still where I saw it on Mount Ararat."

"Good heavens, Hiram. The Ark?"

"Paul, you've been given an opportunity almost no one else has had. You roved the seas on a deck of Noah's Ark."

He had food with him, and he told me his adventures as we lunched upon the sand. I told him all about Grant and Saul and his mother and about the silver fish.

"What you won were skirmishes, Paul. As the saying goes, the battle is never won this side of heaven. What is this place?" He gestured around us.

I told him.

"My prophetic soul warns me it will be important someday. But, come," he said, finishing the last of his sandwich, "let us mount our deck and see if it can be persuaded to float us to your homeland."

"I'm afraid the current doesn't go that way," I said, following him to the platform. "And unless you've fitted it with an outboard motor, we're pretty much committed here until someone sends a boat for us."

"You forget the pedigree, Paul, the pedigree. It goes where it needs to go. What propels it? I have a theory about that giant silver fish you told me of. Ah, well, it is but a theory. Let us get to your village of Ulysses S. Grant—a distinguished name—hopefully in time for supper. I am anxious to meet your friends. And look, Paul. I brought my library, along with an old friend of yours. Behold." It was Stoddard *On the Steam Engine*. "Ho," he said to the deck, "take us, please, to Ulysses S. Grant."

And it did.

Hiram Bell was immediately at home in Grant, he and Tanger

forming a friendship that became the basis of the literary club. Later he formed a different sort of attachment with Belle Zabala. So our community grew and prospered.

Henry and his offspring proved the heroes of the harvest the next year. Our population by then was risen to a hundred eighty-two. By the third year, we numbered three hundred fifty-nine citizens, housed in nearly two hundred separate cottages, some of the larger ones accommodating families of four or six. We have had many marriages; in the first year, eight children were born. Twenty-six children were born in the second year. Sixty-seven the third. So far no one has died.

Thus I bring to a close the first volume of *The History of Our World beyond the Wave,* destined to live as long, Bell assures me, as Herodotus and Gibbon.

We've a lot of recreation even with all the work. Most of us have learned to play the musical instruments found in the library, and there are concerts and dances. We also have sports events and literary and scientific societies. We are partly a nineteenth-century American community and partly a medieval society, with a lot of eighteenth-century England thrown in.

Al the plumber was not much good at doctoring. Fortunately for the community, Wayland Forbes stumbled onto shore one day, and he was a GP. Al was so nettled, he redoubled his medical studies. Together they founded and perpetuate our college of medicine.

Hiram Bell once lamented to me the absence of a priest. He got better than he hoped for. A chartered seaplane that had flown right over the Wave afterwards drifted upon the waters long enough for its occupants to transfer to an abandoned cutter floating nearby. The passengers included twenty-seven bishops back from a conference. The cutter was Tanger's, last seen at Hudson Bay. We also acquired eighteen dogs and a great many more cats.

Our technology may be primitive, but we study the great books in the library, so the rest of our education is superb. Better tech-nology will come, and specialization, when there is time and leisure. On the other hand, we have no crime or other discernible evils, and consider this a fair trade-off. Some of our latest colonists own up to almost biblical life spans. No one has died or even been signifi-cantly ill. Our hard work is more like play. There is a glamour on the land, as though we have regained what we lost long ago. Gone is that bewilderment that accrued throughout history, as of good things silently and wrongfully taken from us, and of the ignoble substituted in their place.

And yet we have reached but another point in time—like the thirteenth century or the Age of Pericles. This is where we are now. Perhaps it too shall pass. In the meantime we savor God's bounty and cherish the day.